DEMONS FOREVER

C.J. HARTNETT

Books by C.J. Hartnett

Demons
Demons in the Night
Demons in my Heart
Demons Forever

DEDICATION

For anyone who found love, and not hate.

ACKNOWLEDGEMENTS

If you are reading this book, thank you. I appreciate all of the support!
Laura Trujillo, thank you for keeping me sane with your words of kindness and Skeletor affirmations and for all the mischief. Thanks to Nicole Hoffmann for making me laugh and for spreading glitter wherever you go. To Christal for being my friend and for your help and advice. To Paige, Gina, Sarah, Bridgette, Carolyn, Kim, Virginia for your advice, support, and friendship.
Thanks to my street team for being so awesome and supportive! You rock!
I would like to thank all of my friends and family for making this possible. Thank you to my sexy man who saved me and kept me strong. You are amazing.

Everyone focuses on pain and revenge. Given the chance, even demons will forget all the pain when love cures them.

PROLOGUE
HARLOW

Watching my prey walk the city streets with confidence brought me joy. It meant that killing him would satisfy the demon inside me. He had murdered young women, almost like he was a Ted Bundy wannabe. It was sick what men did to women, all because they felt they were the superior gender.

I took a deep breath and merged with the rowdy crowd on the sidewalk. Friday night in the city always brought a lot of loud, obnoxious drunks, and somehow, they inevitably found their way to our nightclub, the Downward Spiral.

I purposefully bumped into his shoulder, losing my balance, and fell to the ground.

"Whoa, are you okay?" he asked, helping me to my feet. He was tall, and thin, with dark brown hair that was perfectly short. Clean shaven, and well kept. His blue eyes could mesmerize any woman, but I knew better.

I giggled like a drunk girl. "I'm so sorry. Hard walking in these shoes and drinking." I pointed to my stilettos. I wore a dark blue dress that tightly fit my body.

"I can imagine. I'm Thomas."

"Carrie."

"Nice to meet you. Want me to carry you?"

I laughed and playfully hit his shoulder. "I can walk. Do you live around here?"

His lips stretched into an ominous grin, as if he knew he had his next victim. "Actually, yeah. I got an apartment just up the street. Would you care for a drink?"

"Actually, I've had enough alcohol, but I am starving." I smiled, and I knew he was thinking he'd get laid.

"You're in luck. I have plenty of delectable foods that are sure to whet your appetite."

"Mmm, I bet you do."

He took my hand, and I ached to get over all of it. I was a demon. I enjoyed seeing the fear in people's eyes before I ripped them apart to inhale their life energy. I used to be a human, but that was so long ago, I barely remembered what that was like.

That was the secret. Everyone all thought we were born demons, but demons are made from humans, just like vampires. We were all demons, some of us were just better at hiding than others.

But there were times I just wanted a random kill. Just to see what it was like. And anytime I came across a vampire, I killed them as fast as I could, but that rarely happened. Except recently vampires had come out of hiding, threatening a war.

Thomas brought me to his one-bedroom apartment. It was about the size of my car. He probably paid way too much for it. Turning on the kitchen lights, he turned to me, hunger in his blue eyes.

"Sure you don't want a drink?" Pretty sure that was his way of drugging the girl before raping her and killing her.

He wasn't going to fuck me unless I was passed out, which annoyed me. I seized his throat, and he backed into the refrigerator. He clawed at my hand and I laughed.

"Aww, never met a woman stronger than your weak ass?"

He struggled to breathe as blood rushed to his head.

"Doesn't feel so good, does it?"

Thomas kicked me, but that didn't do anything. That was what I loved most. Seeing them struggle against me. The once so powerful egotistical psychotic was anything but. And in some weird way, he probably got off on it too.

I was bored with him. Knocking him with my elbow, he slid to the ground. I grabbed his head and pulled.

He tried stopping me, but he couldn't overpower me. I kept pulling, stretching his skin until finally it began to break. Blood spurted all over me and the kitchen. As his life escaped, I inhaled every bit of it, letting it fill me. Power charged inside my veins, and once again I felt alive and powerful, and I loved it.

In my former life, I was a timid kitten, afraid of everything, but after watching vampires kill my entire family, and since I'd become a demon, I wasn't afraid of anything. I had made it my goal in life to kill every last vampire. We weren't allowed to show any emotion or feel anything. We were emotionless monsters, trained to kill. Until the Dominus was created. A group of strong demons who created rules that we had to adhere to. Stay within the boundaries, and we could live like normal beings – whatever that was, and if we didn't we paid the price. We could breed. We had jobs. We danced at the club. And once a month, we had a task of killing some poor schmuck that no human would ever miss since they committed crimes. It was a well thought out system. An organized one.

Until one little demon fell in love with a fucking vampire. But she had a killing problem, so maybe being with a vampire actually helped her. She and her lover murdered the Dominus, leaving Trajan, Sawyer, and me as the new Dominus. And now, Trajan had been kidnapped by two fucking vampires who also killed a few demons. Everyone was on edge as to when the vampires would attack next.

Two vampire prisoners had killed several demons and took Trajan with them just a few nights ago. Trajan had been acting strange ever since he became a Dominus member. He seemed hesitant on warring with them, especially after a vampire approached him about becoming a vampire himself. And he actually seemed agreeable to that. Was he so in love with Mina that he wanted to become a vampire, just so they could be together? Seemed like a stretch to me.

But he announced it to the demons, so they knew there was a way to become even stronger than the vampires. And each night we waited, more and more demons left.

I returned to the Lair to check on the army and Sawyer, and to make sure no one got out of line, yet. I wanted to go home but being a member of the Dominus sometimes didn't give me that benefit.

"You're back," Sawyer said. His red hair was unkempt as usual, and he looked exhausted. We all were though. Tired of our kind getting killed or leaving. "Several more demons left."

I let out a frustrated sigh. "Sawyer, we have to do this tonight."

"Should we? If our demons left to become whatever this new breed was, how can we possibly fight them?"

"What is it with you and Trajan? Why are you both so afraid of them? They have done nothing but cause havoc and we need to end it."

"Harlow—"

"I'm so sorry," a man cried as a group of men walked into the Lair. "They overpowered me."

"Indeed," a man with long brown hair spoke. His eyes were black, showing me he was a vampire, but I couldn't smell him or any of his group.

"What do you want?" I demanded, ready for an attack.

"It's really simple. Become a vampire or die."

I laughed. "You're out of your fucking mind if you think I will ever be one of you."

"Suit yourself."

A bomb exploded sending me through the air. My ears rang, and chaos ensued. I fought off as many as I could, but they were much stronger than me. Something was happening to me, like the fumes from the bomb were making me sleepy. No matter how hard I tried, I couldn't keep my eyes open. I was a leader of an army, but in a matter of seconds, I was taken down like I was nothing.

CHAPTER ONE
HARLOW

I was floating. High above the clouds. Weightless. I felt warm, but bits of ice touched my shoulders and knees. It was a strange feeling, but I liked it. I felt safe, like nothing could harm me. The right side of my face throbbed constantly, like my skin had been ripped off.

Even though my mind was in a fog, I remembered a vampire with long brown hair boldly entering the Lair and giving us an ultimatum. Become a hybrid or die. Since vampires had kidnapped Trajan, Sawyer and I did what we thought was right and sent the demons to attack. They had been itching for a war against the hybrids ever since the vampires started kidnapping demons and turning them into hybrids. There were explosions and a war broke out inside the Lair. Or something. I blacked out.

Was I dead? No, I was breathing. Although, I was very weak. I needed to feed. I needed energy.

I wanted to open my eyes, but my right eye refused like my skin had melted together. I tried again, and when I unglued my eyelids, I saw the most beautiful man I'd ever seen. He was carrying me. My eyes roved over his strong, angular face and short dark brown hair that I wanted to run my hands through. When our eyes met, my breath caught in my throat. His emerald eyes captivated me like nothing or no one had ever done, yet I could see pain and sadness. What had caused him to feel such pain? I wanted to take away his pain. Who was this sexy man saving me? And why the hell did I have such a sappy reaction? I was a demon. We thrived on sex and killing. We didn't feel emotions. That wasn't what we were allowed to do.

But that hadn't stopped Mina from falling love with Caleb, a vampire no less. The thought sickened me.

I inhaled, and a powerful scent burned my insides. Alarms rang inside my head. Vampire. His icy arms were holding me. Touching me. Carrying me. Where was I? Was he taking me as prisoner? I pushed away from his body and tumbled to the snowy ground, ready to attack him. A thick forest and several people surrounded us. My eyes were still adjusting, and it was dark, but as I glanced, I swore I recognized one of our previous vampire prisoners. She had killed three of our demons. And as I looked closer at the man who carried me, I recognized him as a vampire prisoner. They had killed demons while held captive and took Trajan with them.

I lunged for the vampire, grasping his neck, but I felt arms wrap around me, pulling me off him. I knew it was stupid to attack, but I had to get away from them. "Get off me," I screamed. "Let me go."

"Harlow, it's okay. He was helping you." I froze once I recognized Trajan's voice. He released me.

"Trajan?" I turned around and there he was. He looked rugged and worn, but somehow stronger than before. His dark hair fell to his shoulders, accentuating his strong facial features. I couldn't believe he was alive and well, standing right before me. "You're alive. I thought you were dead."

"I'm fine. We have to keep moving." His voice was cold and distant, like always.

"Where are we going? What's going on?" As I looked around, I saw several vampires carrying wounded demons, including Sawyer. Had I missed something? Wasn't it the vampires who attacked us? I had seen them rip hearts out of demons like it was nothing. I knew the vampires had been waging a war, and I remembered Trajan mentioning that we could all become hybrids.

"Trajan, these are vampires."

"They're on our side."

I felt sick. Trajan betrayed us, and as I saw the dark headed vampire cling onto him like her life depended on it, it all made sense. He was never in love with Mina, like I had always thought. He was in love with a fucking vampire. That was why he never wanted to war against them. "It was *her* wasn't it? You killed your own kind and left us high and dry for a *vampire*?"

"We'll explain everything when we get to the hideout," Trajan said, but I didn't trust him anymore, given that he left us for a vampire who had killed four demons.

"We're not gonna kill you, if that's what you're worried about," the beautiful vampire with green eyes said. I hated vampires. I hated everything about them, including the creepy translucent skin that made them look like they were dead, except when I stared at the man, I loved the beautiful tone against his rough and weary face. "I know I'm hot, but you can stare at me later," he said, shaking me out of my reverie.

"Fuck you." I moved away from him. He made my skin crawl as if tiny ants pinched every nerve ending. "What the fuck is going on, Trajan? Where have you been?"

"Harlow, I promise we'll explain it all. Come on, we have to keep moving."

"You're siding with *them*?"

"I'm not exactly happy to be siding with the likes of you either but come on," the vampire said. "You need healing."

"Don't tell me what I need." Why was he still talking to me? Who did he think he was? I turned to Trajan. "I can't believe you would betray us. A vampire and his army attacked us. And since Sawyer and I were the only Dominus members left, we did what we had to do. But they…they destroyed everything." I hated how choked up I got, but it was my home away from home. "Vampires killed demons, and you trust them? Did you become one of them?" The words got caught in my throat.

Dmitry moved closer to me, and I was surprised to see him since I thought he had died, too. He was always kind to me, and incredibly hot, but I was never attracted to him like that. "There are more of us," Dmitry said. "I assure you, we'll be fine."

"Look, they had to convince me to come with you demons, but if I can get over my own pride, so can you."

I glared at the vampire, knowing my eyes turned red. "I really don't give a fuck about your pride. We lost our home because of you." I lunged toward him, wanting to rip his heart out, but Dmitry held me back.

"We've all lost our homes," Dmitry said. "Including the vampires. Each of us have lost a lot."

"Why are you sympathetic toward them? If they hadn't attacked us—"

"Harlow!" Trajan yelled. "Stop fucking around. I told you we would explain everything once we got to a safe place. Now come on. We have to get out of here before they find us."

Clenching my fists, I wanted to punch him, but I didn't. If he thought he was still the leader, he had another thing coming. "If whatever you're planning doesn't pan out, I'm out."

My body swayed, and I knew I had exerted too much energy. I was weak from the fight, and my heart pounded against my chest.

"Carry her," Trajan instructed the vampire.

"I'm not your fucking underling, asshole."

The green-eyed vampire apparently felt the same way toward us that I did toward vampires. At least I wasn't alone in that.

"I can walk myself, Trajan. I'm not a weakling."

Trajan threw up his hands. "Then come on before the sun comes up."

Maybe the sun would rise and kill them all. Glancing at the vampire, I wondered why he was even with us if he hated demons.

"Like what you see?" He raised an eyebrow.

"Fuck off." Taking a deep breath, I walked with a strange group of people to somewhere that wasn't home.

CHAPTER TWO
ALARIC

Alaric Kingston didn't give two fucks about that woman. Sure, she was hot, but she was a goddamn demon. Her blonde hair reached the middle of her back, just above her tight ass. Her brown eyes held so much grit, and when they changed to that ruby red it did something to him. Usually, he hated that red eye color, but he didn't carry that hatred when he looked at her.

Whatever. He shook his head. Maybe he was just horny. He would never go for a demon. Plus, she seemed upset that Trajan was with a vampire. Was she in love with him? He rolled his eyes. Why the fuck did he care?

Alaric was giving the group one chance, and that was it. He had only followed them because Grayson turned demons into hybrids and as Alaric escaped the Underground, vampires shot at him. His own kind tried to kill him.

Of course, he also followed the group because of Danielle. True, his ego was bruised and his heart a little broken since she had chosen someone else over him. A demon no less. If that was who she wanted, so be it. Except now, that demon was a hybrid – the same thing they had been trying to kill all goddamn night. They had killed most of them, but Grayson took off like a scared piece of shit. That bastard had killed Alaric's father and most of his coven. The image of his father's detached head from its body haunted him. Every time he closed his eyes, he saw the frozen expression of his father's face. By now, they were all ashes.

Alaric didn't know where the rest of the vampires or hybrids were, but he swore he'd kill every single one of those hybrids once he found them.

When they reached the hideout, just before sunrise, they each claimed a room like it was a fucking Holiday Inn. The injured demons were placed in their own room. He didn't know how they healed, if it was like vampires, but he didn't care. Being that Alaric was single, or whatever the fuck, he was about the only one not fucking in their bedroom. He needed something to take the edge off. He needed to feed, but since the demons or hybrids or whatever the fuck they were, killed just about everything in sight, he was limited. Humans were far away from this place, and he should be glad that it was so remote. He was tired and needed to rest.

The hideout, or lodge, was quiet, and he missed the noise of the Underground. He missed the vast windows of his loft that overlooked the city. Alaric and his coven had only come to Danielle's coven to bring order, since Caleb, the vampire king, was M.I.A. They knew someone was on the inside planning something. Had his coven never come to the godforsaken city, they'd all still be alive, Alaric never would have met Danielle, and he sure as shit wouldn't have been hiding out with a bunch of demons.

He thought about returning home, but there wasn't much point since his coven was dead or missing. His original home was right on the river in the middle of a city. It was a perfect spot to find tourists and give them a taste of the city, and more. He didn't know if he would ever be able to return.

Alaric didn't know what they were going to do. It had been a long night. A long and painful night. As he settled in a chair next to the window, he looked out at the dark forest and the snow that covered it. Closing his eyes, he saw his father's decapitated head like it was seared to his mind. Ezra wasn't really his father, but since Alaric had joined the coven, he was. Ezra always treated him as a son. Sonya, Flynn, Erika, Sebastian. They were all his siblings for all intents and purposes, but now they were gone. Every single one of them.

What the fuck was Grayson doing? He became the vampire King. What more did he want? What was the purpose in creating hybrids? Demons were just emotionless killing machines and making them into vampires only seemed to make them the ultimate weapon.

Alaric needed a drink. He made his way down the stairs hoping the kitchen would be empty, and to his luck, it was. He pulled out a small glass and a bottle of whiskey from the cabinets. Thankfully there was plenty of it. He poured himself a shot and downed it.

Leaning against the long island in the kitchen, he looked around at the black granite counters and white cabinets. He had no idea who built the place, but it felt weird. A few minutes later, the blonde demon appeared and grabbed a glass.

He poured her some whiskey and refilled his glass.

He kept glancing at the demon. Half her face had been burned, and she looked like she was about to faint. Shouldn't she have healed by now? He didn't know how to help them and didn't know why he would want to save them.

He refilled their glasses with a little whiskey. "For what it's worth, I agree with you."

"What the fuck do you agree with?"

"That if this whole plan doesn't pan out, you're out."

"You only agree with me because you want in my pants." She sipped her drink and challenged him with her large eyes.

Challenge accepted. "One, I can get into your pants anytime, but I wouldn't because of what you are. Two, I agree with you because you're right."

She downed her drink.

"It seems a bit strange to me that this group came together."

"Given that some vampire has Trajan's balls wrapped around her finger, it doesn't surprise me."

"I sense some hostile jealousy. Were you and Trajan…?"

She lifted an eyebrow. "Yeah, I'm head over heels madly in love with that asshole. It's because he left everything in shambles because of a vampire. He gave up everything and left us. He should be punished."

"Like you punished Danielle and me in your depressing cellar?" He hadn't forgotten they had kidnapped the two of them and tortured them. Alaric was sick of demons and their torture.

She shrugged. "What do you expect. Vampires are ruthless monsters who deserve to die."

Alaric moved closer to her, towering over her, but she didn't flinch one bit. "Not all vampires are bad."

Her brown eyes glared at him as she straightened her stance. "I could kill you in two seconds."

He let out a chuckle. "What's stopping you?"

Harlow squinted her eyes, and swayed slightly, catching herself on the island counter. "What the fuck did you give me?"

"It's whiskey, but you look like shit so maybe you need to rest like the rest of the house. Your face hasn't healed."

"Yeah, I'm aware of that, no thanks to your kind. I bet you were in on it, following that prick's orders. Just had to come tail us and report back to him."

"Believe what you want." He drank the last of the whiskey from his glass and walked away. She was definitely a paranoid demon who needed therapy. If that was even a thing. But he understood her anger, because he felt the same way. A vampire, someone of his own kind, had killed his entire coven and demons. He felt betrayed, but he knew if things didn't work out with the group, he'd find a way to kill Grayson, even if it meant dying in the process.

CHAPTER THREE
HARLOW

Standing in the foyer of the massive hideout, it felt more like a weekend getaway in the mountains. Three couches filled the living room in a U-shape with a fireplace at the center of the room. In the back was a staircase that turned and led to bedrooms. Even though the walls were made of wood, I was cold, which wasn't a good sign. We didn't get cold, and my face still throbbed. I wasn't healing, but I just needed to feed. And I needed a quick fuck, so I could gain strength, but I was exhausted and weak.

As everyone gathered in the main room, I kept glancing at the man with the beautiful, haunting green eyes. The one who carried me to safety. A vampire saved a demon. Since when had that ever happened? There was an air of arrogance about him, yet I detected sorrow. Even still, he made my skin crawl.

As I looked around the room, I saw things that were foreign to me. Things that had always been ingrained inside me as forbidden. I saw Mina, a demon, romantically caress Caleb, a vampire. Trajan, a demon, kiss Danielle, a vampire's temple. I didn't miss the way the stranger clenched his teeth and looked away. Maybe he was just as disgusted as I was at the sight. Like that fucking vampire hadn't caused enough issues. She had Trajan wrapped around her little finger, and now he was a hybrid.

Then there was Dmitry, a demon who for whatever reason, brought in a fucking human of all things. What had happened to us? Why had I been so out of the loop? Was there a witch spreading love spells with everyone? Demons and vampires did not coexist on friendly terms. They never had.

Sawyer, Estrella, and London, other demons who were found at the Lair, sat together on a couch. Sawyer's leg shook as he bit his lip. Maybe being in a room of vampires made him nervous, but something else was definitely on his mind. Both he and Trajan had been acting preoccupied before the war. My eyes returned to Danielle and Trajan.

I shivered and grew impatient with the lovebirds. "Let me get this straight." They all turned to me. "Mina and Caleb killed the original Dominus. Trajan killed some of our men because they tortured Danielle and left us behind for her. Dmitry went rogue and Caleb didn't want to be the king of vampires, so they gave it to some psycho vampire, who in turn decided to make fucking hybrids. And now we're having to fight this asshole?"

"That's the gist," Danielle said in an Australian accent. She was tall with dark hair and eyes, and as she eyed me, I knew she was judging me wondering if I truly belonged there. "We did these things for love."

"Yeah, your love started a fucking war."

"I don't expect you to fully grasp the idea of love."

"What's that supposed to mean?" I clenched my teeth, wanting to rip her head off, but I shivered again, losing more strength.

"Okay, no fighting," Trajan said, standing in front of the blazing fireplace. I stood nearby, trying to keep warm. I had respected him my entire life, but lately with the secrets and lies, my respect for him diminished. While every woman clung to his every word because of his incredibly good looks, I saw Trajan for who he really was, and he liked that I didn't fawn all over him. He was my friend, and I never thought of him as more. Sadly, I didn't know who he was anymore.

"We're all friends here," Trajan said, and my vampire savior scoffed. I didn't blame him. "We need to fight Grayson."

"Didn't this Grayson guy say that creating demons was a mistake?" I asked. "Then why is he mixing breeds?"

"Probably because you are an emotionless breed and—"

I snapped my head in the stranger's direction. "Don't for one second think we don't carry emotions."

He sighed. "It's because of your lack of emotions and strength, you mix that with vampire strength and speed, you create the ultimate killing breed."

Everyone turned to him. He seemed to know a lot more than he led on. What else did he know? Was he a spy for Grayson? It didn't make sense for him to be here, unless he was in love with Danielle by the way he stared at her. But every so often, I caught him glancing at me.

"Alaric's right," Trajan said. My stomach did a weird flip once I learned my savior's name. Alaric. It fit him. "Except I don't feel any different aside from the vast strength and the sudden blood lust," Trajan continued.

I didn't miss Dmitry's human shrink behind him, but I knew she was safe. Dmitry was a protector, and he'd kill anything or anyone for getting too close to his loved ones.

"How did Grayson know where to find the Lair?" I asked.

"Trajan may have sold you out," Alaric said.

Trajan squared his shoulders. "You got something to say?"

"All I know is you were the one making deals with Grayson. He turned you into a hybrid for a reason."

I turned to Trajan. "Is that what you did? You told the demons they could become hybrids, so a lot of them left the Lair. Now they're our enemies. How did they find the Underground?"

Danielle sighed. "It had to be Caroline working with Grayson."

"Caroline was not working with Grayson," Sawyer said through clenched teeth.

Everyone looked at him.

"And how do you know that?" I asked.

Sawyer stood. His red hair was disheveled, as usual, and his brown eyes looked sad. "Because I'm in love with her. And she would never sell me out."

"Then why wouldn't she escape with me and Trajan?" Danielle questioned.

"We were planning to leave all of this. When Grayson and his men shot up the demons that night, we ran, but we lost track of each other. I came back to the Lair to warn Harlow. I never found Caroline."

Danielle stared at him like she didn't believe him. "I didn't see her in the rubble at the Underground, and I searched."

Sawyer shook his head. "She wouldn't have betrayed us. She loves me. And she's your best friend. How could you think she betrayed you?"

"She was acting strange that night before the attack."

"I find it hard to believe that a vampire could ever love a demon," Alaric said, and I agreed. But I also found it difficult to understand how a demon could love a vampire. The whole idea was ridiculous. And it pissed me off that two of the Dominus members were going to up and leave me and their kind. For vampires.

"It happens," Caleb said. His dirty blond hair was unkempt, and he looked exhausted, like everyone else. The vampire King stood amongst us and didn't look at us in disgust. He stayed close to Mina. It was strange to see her with him, considering she had pined for Trajan for years, but watching the two of them together made sense. They were both outcasts in a way, and since Mina could never have sex without killing someone, she had met her match. Still, the thought of even touching a vampire revolted me.

Dmitry cleared his throat. "There's something you all should know. Aria is a demon and a human."

"What?" I stared at him. "Are you fucking kidding me? How is that even possible? Are there no pure breeds anymore?"

"I kept feeding her my energy, and now she's half demon. And the witches are after her."

"Witches?" Alaric shook his head. "Why are they after her?"

"We don't know."

Aria was incredibly timid as they came. She held onto Dmitry tightly. Glancing at Alaric, I could see the vein in his neck bulging. His eyes were black as night. He was hungry. They all were.

Trajan stood from the couch acting like the leader of the group. "I'm not sure how any of this is possible. We need to convince the demons and other vampire covens to help."

I crossed my arms in front of my chest. "You're kidding, right? After you bailed on your own kind, you think demons would ever listen to you again? Besides, they're all dead now."

He sighed. "Not all of them."

"You think we're supposed to convince the demons to fight alongside vampires after what they've done to us? They made the majority of us into hybrids without choice." Among other things that I'd rather not remember. I shivered again, feeling the weakness even more.

"They had a choice."

"Yeah because you led them to it!"

"Look, each side has done things to each other," he said. "We have to work with each other if we want to win and regain our home."

"We have no home anymore, Trajan," I reminded him.

"We can rebuild, Harlow. It's just going to take all of us working together."

I rolled my eyes.

The night was full of surprises. I was tired, and I needed energy.

"I think we all need to rest and talk tomorrow about what we're going to do," Trajan said. No one seemed to mind at all. They all stood, and each couple went into their own rooms, probably to have lots of sex. Except Alaric.

I trembled again, but I needed to feed. I needed power. I needed to find some poor sap to fuck to regain my powers.

CHAPTER FOUR
ALARIC

A fire blazed in the fireplace like it was some cozy cabin for lovers. Alaric hated seeing Danielle and Trajan together. Seeing that fucking demon hybrid touch her made his skin crawl. He had to move on.

Sighing, he opened the door and made his way out into the cold night. Fucking drama. He still wasn't sure about being with the group of mixed breeds. He couldn't believe Aria was a demon and human. What exactly did that mean to her? Why even get humans involved? And witches had been added to the mix. Vampires betraying their own kind. Demons seeking more power, of course. Could it have gotten any more fucked up?

Alaric was hungry and all he had been smelling for the last several hours was expired human blood and demons. He couldn't stand it. As he walked in the snow, he stopped once he heard something. He caught a whiff of rich, warm blood and raced toward it. His fangs were out, and his heart pumped with the need.

He reached the body but halted once he saw Harlow, the sexy blonde demon hovering over a bloody human. His head had been ripped from his body, like some gore fest. She was covered in blood. Fucking demons never did anything clean. "Goddammit."

She snapped her head toward him and her eyes were a ruby red. For some reason it didn't turn him off or give him nightmares. It actually turned him on. "What do you want?" she spat.

The sweet scent of the blood spilling out of the human made his mouth water. "I need to feed."

Glaring at him for a minute, she gave a disgusted sound and pushed the body toward him. "Have at it." She got to her feet.

Taking the body, he sank his teeth in the human. The blood was still fresh, thankfully, and tasted sweet. It helped take the edge off, but not enough. He needed more blood. He looked up and saw a cabin.

"Was he the only one?"

She nodded. "He was getting firewood."

"Damn."

"Maybe next time I'll wait," Harlow said, watching him.

Alaric wiped his mouth and stood. "Are you apologizing?"

"Look, I don't want to be in this situation any more than you. I fucking hate vampires, but it looks like our group is the only one willing to fight against the hybrids. And you did save me."

Something stirred inside him as she spoke. Her hatred and anger was hot, but he noticed a small part of her soften. Maybe demons had souls after all. Who knew?

"Maybe. Unless your group is really just luring us in to kill us. I've never trusted demons."

She cocked an eyebrow and her eyes became brown. "Trajan betrayed his own kind for vampires, so no, we aren't luring you anywhere. Though I can imagine you trust demons even less now that your girl chose Trajan."

Clenching his teeth, he rushed up to her, but she didn't flinch. She wasn't afraid of him at all. He wasn't used to that.

Most demons shrank away from him. And for whatever reason, Alaric didn't want her to fear him. "You don't know what the fuck you're talking about."

They stood face to face, both panting, staring into each other's eyes. She smelled like blood, yet there was a faint scent of jasmine. As he stared into her eyes, he felt the strangest feeling. She didn't look like a demon, and even though she tried holding a glare, she showed a yearning.

The world was coming to an end, and there Alaric was thinking about fucking a demon. His dick was hard and throbbing as he had visions of fucking her against the tree. Imagining how warm she would feel around him.

He shook his head. She was a *demon.*

She stared at him with the same heated gaze. He wanted to rip every piece of clothing off her. No one would know. No one would see. It was dark in the woods, only a sliver of moonlight reflected off the snow. Besides, he'd be helping her out. She needed power.

"Are we gonna stare at each other all night or are you gonna fight me? Isn't that what you want?"

"I don't want to fight. I want to fuck you," he blurted.

"Then what are you waiting for?"

That was all he needed. His mouth claimed hers with a hot kiss. Alaric tore her shirt open and his hands wandered over her soft skin. Her breasts were perfect, her nipples erect. Fire consumed his body as she ripped his shirt and removed his jeans. Every touch, every kiss, felt like trails of sultry heat all over him. Removing her jeans, he lifted her, wrapping her legs around his waist, and slid his hard cock slowly into her wet warmth. Inch by inch. He let out a long moan. She was incredibly tight. Nothing had ever felt so good. It was like his first time. His dick throbbed inside her, and he stayed there for a second until she started to squirm. Pulling out a little, he slammed into her. Goddamn she felt amazing. He could feel her pussy clenching around his cock and he loved feeling her arms tight around him as her breasts rubbed against his bare chest.

As he pushed inside her again and again, she panted into his ear, gripping his hair. She cried out so loud, and for a second, he feared someone would hear, but he didn't care. Let the world know he caused this beautiful woman to scream.

"You're so fucking wet," he whispered.

"Shut the fuck up." She ran her tongue over his ear and bit his lobe making his cock pulse harder.

It had never felt like that for him, like everything was right. He wanted it to last forever. Leaning down a bit, he seized her nipple in his mouth and gently bit it causing her to moan. He liked hearing her breathless sounds and wanted to hear more.

"Harder," she moaned as her eyes turned red.

That mesmerizing ruby color caused his blood to simmer. He slammed into her hard and her breath caught as she leaned her head against the tree. He pumped into her so hard that snow from the tree branches fell on them encasing them in brief intervals of cold. Alaric couldn't hold back much longer, and a hiss ripped from his lips as he emptied his seed into the sexy demon.

After a few seconds, he pulled out of her, and the bitter cold replaced the warmth and tension between them. As she stood there, he couldn't help but enjoy the sexy way her chest filled as she breathed, making her breasts rise. He wanted to touch her soft skin again. Wanted to hear her moan and scream. Wanted to feel her warmth.

Alaric shook his head. He was just horny, that was all. But he couldn't stop gazing into her eyes that had returned to their chocolate color. Her face had slowly begun to heal, but she still looked pale. Was she okay? Did demons usually take a while to heal? Why the fuck did he even care about a goddamn demon?

CHAPTER FIVE
HARLOW

As I leaned against the tree, I hated how empty I felt the second Alaric pulled out of me. His eyes pinned mine, and I hated that I couldn't look away. He was beautiful, especially naked. The clean lines on his chest and abs and groin made my heart sputter. I couldn't believe my reactions to him, let alone what I had just allowed to happen. It had never felt like that before. Like I was complete. I had never felt so incredible and my legs shook. No one had ever made me come three times, especially from a quickie. He definitely knew how to make a woman feel.

But he was a vampire. A fucking gorgeous amazing-in-bed vampire.

I shook my head. It was a one-time thing. I needed power, that was all it was. I wasn't attracted to him at all. We had both experienced tragedies as both our homes were destroyed, and friends and family were killed and needed to feel a little closeness. It was amazing nevertheless.

"Is your back okay? It looks scratched," Alaric said.

I replaced my shirt and smirked. "It'll heal." A sharp pain hit my head and I swayed as a wave of dizziness fell on me.

"Are you okay?" He moved closer, and my breath hitched. A strange buzz of excitement consumed me, and I hated that he caused it.

"I'm fine."

"I know I'm amazing in bed but can't say I ever made a woman weak in the knees."

"I need to go." The throbbing pain took over and wouldn't stop. I didn't know what the fuck I just did. I fucked a goddamn vampire. Was this what happened when demons hooked up with vampires?

"Do you need any help?"

Letting out an annoyed sigh, I turned away from him. "I'm not weak. I can take care of myself."

Walking back in the snow, I couldn't keep warm. I had fed and had sex, and it still wasn't enough. I wanted to feed more, but I knew what happened to demons who overindulged too quickly. Maybe sleep would help. The whole way back to the lodge, I thought of how amazing Alaric felt inside me, and what he looked like under all the clothes and the thick exterior.

I shook my head.

Why the fuck did I care? I couldn't believe I had fucked a vampire, but I was desperate. However, I always felt incredibly stronger after I had sex, but I still felt the same weakness. But sex had never felt that amazing. Something was really wrong with me if I thought that.

Once I reached the house, I went straight to the kitchen, glad that no one was downstairs. I needed a drink. I could still smell him on me, a woodsy scent mixed with the salty ocean. It was unique, especially for a vampire.

Vampires were ice cold, but the way Alaric touched me set my entire body on fire. Thinking about his long, hard cock pumping in and out of me had my heart racing again. I poured a shot of whiskey and downed it. I needed to calm down. I was in trouble. Was this how Mina felt about Caleb? Or Trajan about Danielle? Sawyer and Caroline? It was what started this war. I drank another shot and headed upstairs.

I chose the room at the very end of the hall because it was quiet, and it was next to an empty room. I didn't want to be near any of the couples. Curling up under the blankets on the bed, I closed my eyes.

It was all so human. Thinking about being with someone like that. It was a one-time thing. I couldn't think like that. Demons weren't programmed for that nonsense.

However, because everyone decided they were in love with mixed breeds, it left everyone in the hands of some maniacal vampire, who in turn blew up the Lair, killing a vast majority of demons, and destroyed the Underground, killing vampires. Love made people weak. It made them lose focus on what really mattered.

And here we were, demons, vampires, and hybrids joining forces to kill a growing army of psychotic hybrids. I guessed demons and vampires shouldn't exist, but who was to say hybrids should?

Sleep evaded me, and I made my way downstairs to the main room to the warm fireplace. A fire still lazily burned, and I pulled a blanket around me, sitting in front of the fire. No matter what, I was still cold. I had never felt anything like it and it scared me. I hated feeling like that. There was only one other time in my life that I felt that scared. Vampires had captured me and used me as a science experiment. They had taken my blood, starved me, and kept me in the dark for weeks. They freed me, probably expecting me to die. I vowed I would never be a prisoner again, but there I was cold as the night, while everyone else was warm and in bed. Maybe this was how I died. By some bizarre circumstance. It couldn't have been the bomb that had gone off in the Lair. I had no idea what was wrong with me, but I wanted it to end. The throbbing, almost debilitating pain. The weakness. The cold. All of it.

CHAPTER SIX
ALARIC

Sleep wasn't happening as Alaric had tossed and turned enough that night. He'd had a weak moment in the woods with Harlow, but admittedly, she was hot as fuck, and thinking about the way her wet pussy felt around his cock, made it throb again. It was a onetime thing, but he couldn't stop thinking about her. Maybe he did Harlow a service since sex made them stronger. He had to admit. He loved her fire and loved how she thought, because he felt the same fucking way.

He hated watching her walk away from him, but she didn't want him around. When he had returned to the cabin, he peeked inside her room and found her sleeping. He told himself he just wanted to see if she made it back okay and that he didn't need a group of demons accusing him of anything that may have happened to her.

Peering out the window, he decided to go for a walk. He dressed, and when he opened his door, he was relieved not to hear any sounds. He'd heard enough squeaking beds and moans all night long. As he reached the last step on the stairs, he spotted something out of the corner of his eye.

Alaric turned and saw Harlow, face down in front of the fireplace. What a strange way to sleep, but he realized upon closer observation, she wasn't moving.

"Harlow?"

Nothing.

Fuck.

Lunging for her, he lifted her cold body into his lap and slapped her face.

Nothing.

"Harlow!"

He didn't know what to do and wasn't sure why he cared. Biting into his wrist, he pressed his bleeding arm to her lips coaxing her to drink. He didn't know how to heal demons if they could be healed. Most of them were torturous monsters. He knew how to kill them. That was all he had cared to know. Holding her, he felt something. He didn't know what though. Something strange he had never felt before, not even with Dani. It was as if he ached for her to wake, and the unease zooming throughout him if she didn't.

Alaric felt her mouth move, her lips tickled his wrist as she began to slowly suck his blood.

Harlow's eyes opened, the most beautiful ruby red, and he felt a strange relief. He loved the way she stared at him while she drank. When she had enough, she pulled away.

"Well that answers that."

"Answers what," she asked, but her voice was all wrong. It was hoarse. What had happened to her at that Lair?

"How to heal a demon. I've only known how to kill your kind."

"Yet, we're the ruthless ones."

"I didn't have to help."

"But you did."

"Only because our friends seem to trust each other for some fucked up reason."

"If you don't want to be here, then leave." She removed herself from his arms and lap, and for a second, he felt a twinge of hollowness.

Harlow stood, and stumbled. Alaric caught her before she fell. Had something happened to her in that explosion or the battle that no one knew about? Could demons get sick? Her skin tone was almost the same as his, and she was cold. Her eyes were no longer ruby, but a beautiful, expressive brown.

"I can't walk." Her body went slack, and he lifted her into his arms.

She coughed, spraying blood. Turning her head away from him, and blood spewed from her mouth. He eased her down and held her hair back until she was finished.

Fuck. Was vampire blood toxic to demons? Alaric carefully placed her on the couch, his heart racing. Stroking her hair, he wanted to comfort her and help her, but didn't know how. He wanted his blood to save her, and a small part of his ego was wounded that it obviously hadn't. It worsened her condition.

"What the fuck is going on out here?" Trajan barreled down the stairs, and when he entered the room, Alaric stood. "What did you do to her?"

"She was sick. I tried helping her," he said as Dani joined Trajan.

"Did you feed her your blood?" Trajan asked. "We aren't vampires, asshole."

He wanted to punch Trajan, but he held back. Harlow needed help first. And fast.

Trajan picked her up. "She's weak and needs to feed more."

"I'll take her," Alaric offered.

"You've done enough harm." He pushed past him and left carrying Harlow in his arms.

Fine. Let the demons deal with their shit. Like he cared. He made his way to the kitchen for a drink. After swallowing a shot of whiskey, he felt Dani behind him. "What?"

She touched his arm and he flinched, removing it from her. "Are you okay?"

"I'm fucking fantastic."

She sighed. "Why won't you let anyone in?"

"You're fucking joking, right? Like it would've made a difference, Dani." Shaking his head, he grabbed the liquor bottle and walked out. Why the fuck did she care about him? She chose a demon over him. A demon who had left her in the dust ages ago, and she took him back. But if that was who she wanted, so be it.

Inside his quaint room, he kept the lights off, and made his way to the chair next to the window. The brilliant light of the moon illuminated the room just enough. He needed to feed, but he didn't feel like it. For whatever reason, he kept thinking of Harlow and wondered if she was okay. He didn't know why he cared so much, but he did. Alaric didn't want to be responsible for her death, but he also longed to see those eyes again.

CHAPTER SEVEN
HARLOW

After draining the life from my third victim, I began to feel normal. I didn't even rip my victims to shred, like I loved doing, but I was too frail. Trajan had brought me out to the nearest town with humans. I couldn't remember what had just happened, though. Everything was hazy, but I remember seeing Alaric's eyes. Unless I dreamed that. No, he was there, calling my name, trying to wake me. He was trying to help me.

"I don't know if Alaric can be trusted," Trajan said as if he read my mind. Only vampires could do that, but he was a hybrid. Could he read minds?

"Why? Because you think he's gonna steal Danielle away from you?"

"This has nothing to do with her. He just tried to kill you."

"What? That's not what happened." Trajan and his paranoia. He had always cared about what people thought of him rather than follow his true feelings, until recently. I guessed that was why he finally decided to get back with Danielle, but he was still a jealous, paranoid demon. And now that he was also a vampire, his senses were heightened, which meant his jealousy and paranoia were out of whack.

He glared at me. "Are you sure you know what happened back there?"

"He tried helping me."

"Alaric fed you his blood. And you threw it up. He had to ingest something before, so you'd drink it. I've drank vampire blood and the only thing that happened was it made me stronger."

That sobered me up. "What?" Vampires were always coming up with ways to slyly kill demons. I hated vampires, but Alaric started to seem different. Had he made his blood toxic to me? Why would he do that knowing everyone in that lodge would kill him? Unless in some sick twisted way that was what he wanted. But why did I throw it up? Why was my body rejecting everything? What had those sick hybrids done to me at the Lair?

"Yeah. Let that sink in."

Trajan was a dick. Ever since he deserted us for a vampire. Fuck him if he thought I was going to let him have the upper hand.

"You brought them here, Trajan. What made you think you could trust them?"

"Harlow, I know how you feel about vampires—"

"I wonder why that is. Yet we're staying in a house full of them and all of you are vampire sympathizers. One of them tried to kill me. You killed your own kind. What happened to you?"

"The demons I killed tortured Dani. If you understood love, you'd know why I did that." His words stung a little. "Not all vampires are our enemies."

"Sure. They turned you into a hybrid, and one tried to kill me."

"I know that, and I'll fix it. We need to do what we can to stick together, Harlow. We have such a small group and we're all in this. We all want the same thing."

"Who's to say these vampires aren't fucking with us? They're manipulative and have you all wrapped around their fingers. All of you are so blinded by this ridiculous notion of love. It doesn't exist, Trajan. Especially between vampires and demons. It's like witches got a hold of your minds or the vampires have compelled you."

"You know we can't be compelled. And I know you feel this way, but demons do feel love. It's possible. Everything we were ever taught before the original Dominus was wrong. We feel things, and one day you'll see."

"Highly doubtful."

"Just don't kill anyone."

"Oh, so it's okay for them to kill me, but god forbid we touch anyone? You just said you didn't know if you could trust him. He just tried to kill me. And now he's in that cabin with Danielle. Maybe she thinks you care for me more. Or maybe she realizes she loves Alaric and wants him. They could be conspiring against us. Maybe she chose you as a ruse."

Trajan set his jaw as his dark eyes glared at me. Got him. He turned back toward the lodge and took off. What a jealous ass. Danielle had chosen him, a demon. Not someone of her own kind. Wasn't that good enough for him? Was he really that afraid of her going back to Alaric, or was he truly worried that Alaric fed me his blood? Why was he so threatened by Alaric? Trajan was a fucking hybrid. He could take down any one of us.

But I understood his paranoia. It made sense if Alaric really was on the inside. He hated being there with us and expressed it numerous times. Was he trying to slaughter us one by one? He could've been playing nice to me all while really trying to kill me. But he could've killed me in the woods earlier. No one was around.

By the time I returned, the lodge was quiet for once. I passed Alaric's room on the way to mine, and briefly thought about stopping to confront him, but I didn't. I went to my room and let exhaustion take over.

CHAPTER EIGHT
ALARIC

He didn't want to feel like a creeper, but he had to know if Harlow was okay. Sneaking into her room, he watched her sleep so peacefully. Her color had returned, and she looked beautiful. The sun filtered through the windows illuminating her golden hair. She was the epitome of a sleeping beauty. A small part of him was jealous that she could feel the warmth of the sun, however, Alaric had found out the glass for the windows were made for vampires, so it blocked the rays. He guessed Trajan did that when he and Dani frequented the place.

When Harlow opened her eyes, and saw him, she jumped, ready for an attack. "What the fuck are you doing in here?"

Alaric held up his hands. "I just wanted to see if you were okay."

"Wanted to finish the job?"

"Despite what it looks like, I didn't hurt you on purpose."

"Is that your vampire compulsion trying to work?"

He sighed. "No, I can't compel you and you know that. I'm sorry. I didn't know my blood was toxic to you."

She let out a hard laugh. "That's a lie. You did something to it, didn't you? You tried to kill me. Why are you even here? Ever since you got here you've questioned everything."

"And you haven't?"

"At least I haven't tried killing anyone. You're on Grayson's side, aren't you?"

He clenched his teeth but loosened them. "I'm glad to know you're okay and that I didn't kill you. I'll leave now." He knew Trajan had turned her against him.

He slammed the door on his way out. It seemed as though no matter where he went, he was the bad guy. Vampires shot at him as he escaped the Underground. Demons deserted the Lair to become hybrids. Too many people betrayed each other, and no one trusted anyone. He knew Trajan had turned Harlow against him, as he'd been trying to oust him as a bad guy since the day he met Alaric. How would they even go to war with Grayson since it was obvious the group couldn't even work together? Grayson had an army, willing to do whatever he wanted. It was organized and there wasn't any drama. He'd even supplied his army with guns to shoot demons and vampires.

Alaric let out a sigh. The group was severely outnumbered and unprepared. And if Trajan was going to lead the group, they definitely had zero chance of winning anything. He was too concerned with his own self to notice what was really happening. Alaric was glad Harlow was alive, but he couldn't take much more of the fucked-up shit that went on in the group.

But he also didn't want to leave. He didn't know why, but he felt protective of Harlow.

CHAPTER NINE
HARLOW

Watching Alaric leave my room did something to me. I hated him for what he did, but I didn't, because somewhere deep down inside I knew he wasn't lying. I was too weak to detect his lying, but I saw it in his eyes. Granted, vampires had a way to hide things. Maybe his blood had some magic that made me feel this way toward him.

I knew Trajan wouldn't want Alaric around much longer, which was fine by me. But somewhere inside me, I knew that wasn't true. I didn't want him to leave, and I didn't want Trajan to banish him.

I grabbed my head and let out a frustrated groan. "What is wrong with me?" I couldn't like a vampire. Not after everything they had done to me. Not after he poisoned his blood and forced me to drink it. Were all the vampires in on the sick game?

After taking a hot shower, I dressed and met everyone downstairs. A fire blazed in the fireplace, and the three couples had taken residence on the couches while Alaric and I stood nearby. Sawyer, Estrella, and London sat together, watching everyone else in the room, like any second someone was going to attack. I wanted to be near the fire, but I didn't want to go near Alaric. His simple blue shirt and jeans hugged his body in a sexy way. I hated that I thought that. Why was it that the nice girls were always attracted to the bad boys? Was it because the boys dripped confidence? They weren't shy and knew what they wanted. Attractive or not, he was a vampire who had tried to kill me. Whether it was really an accident or not will perhaps remain a mystery.

"I'm so glad you're feeling better, Harlow," Danielle said, curled up next to Trajan.

"I'm sure you are." I crossed my arms in front of my chest.

"Harlow," Trajan warned, and got to his feet. "Before we begin, I'm sure you all know last night, one of our own was severely injured by Alaric. He fed Harlow his blood and she threw it up. I believe he tampered with his blood before he fed it to her. He claims he is unaware that his blood was toxic. We all need to decide if he stays or goes."

"You can talk to me instead of referring to me in the third person."

"Alright then. Are you an imposter?"

"Jesus, Trajan, knock it off," Danielle said. "You aren't a Dominus member anymore."

She spoke as if the Dominus was just some insignificant group. She had no idea what being a Dominus meant, and obviously she didn't care. "Just because our Lair was destroyed, doesn't mean the Dominus doesn't exist."

Danielle raised an eyebrow. "Either way, the Dominus can't decide the fate of vampires. Alaric didn't do anything to his blood. He was simply trying to save you."

"Whatever. He's been miserable since he got here. He doesn't want to be here." It was true, but some part of me held on to the fact that he was good, and I didn't know why.

Alaric chuckled. "If you all want to believe that I'm on Grayson's side, so be it. I really don't give two fucks what you think."

Trajan squared his shoulders. "You're a spy for him? I mean, you showed up here conveniently after the fight at the Underground."

"For fucks sake, Trajan," Danielle shouted.

"I like that you feel so threatened by me." Alaric challenged Trajan. "It's quite entertaining. Still believe Dani's better off with me and that she'll come back?"

Trajan drove his fist into Alaric's chin. Alaric tackled him to the ground. As they grappled around on the floor, I couldn't help but feel a little jealous that it was all over Danielle. What was so special about her anyway? Was she that good in bed?

Caleb and Dmitry pulled the primates apart, all of them breathing hard.

"Look, the animosity has to stop between all of us," Dmitry said, his voice overpowered any other sound. "We're never going to accomplish a goddamn thing if we can't stop going at each other's throats. Alaric was trying to help Harlow. He made a mistake. I'm fairly certain he never learned how to save a demon. Same reason we never learned how to save vampires. We know how to kill each other. Now, we can learn to save each other. Maybe Harlow threw up the blood because she was too weak to take it. End of story." He ran a hand through his long hair and gave a frustrated sigh.

"That was no mistake," Trajan said. "He knew exactly what he was doing."

Alaric shook his head. "You want me gone? So be it."

"Alaric, no," Danielle said, but he was already at the door.

"Only a guilty man would've done that," Trajan said.

Words caught in my throat, and I couldn't stop him. I wouldn't know how. I didn't want him to leave. I believed him when he told me he hadn't meant for his blood to harm me, and I hated myself for not speaking up. Bits and pieces of that night came back to me slowly. Danielle ran after him, but I wanted to be the one, and sadly, a small part of my heart sank.

Fuck. What was wrong with me?

"Dani, wait!" Trajan followed her.

"Jesus fuck it's like fucking high school in here," Caleb said. "Do they not understand the severity of our situation?"

London chuckled. "Pretty sure a lot of us have never been to high school. We were made demons too early."

Estrella grabbed his hand and smiled at him. Her copper hair almost reached her elbows in long curls. I always wanted to be a redhead, and I wasn't sure why I never colored my hair.

"We need to figure something out, because I have to find Caroline," Sawyer said.

I plopped down on the couch. "We're not going to make it if Trajan keeps fucking us over. He's not a good leader. He's too wrapped up with Danielle to focus on anything else."

"What do you suggest?" Dmitry asked, as he held Aria's hand.

"You. You've always been a good decision-maker. You're not an arrogant dick."

Mina raised an eyebrow. "I thought you were Trajan's best friend."

I rolled my eyes. "Trajan's dick is his best friend. Come on, D. Sawyer and I need you."

"Harlow, why not you? When the original Dominus died, you took care of shit. We all know it wasn't just Trajan leading."

"He was too busy dealing with Danielle and keeping her safe."

"Exactly. But you're smart and you don't take anyone's shit. You and Sawyer were part of the new Dominus."

"That didn't work out so well," Sawyer said. "Seeing as how we tried to fight Grayson and lost miserably."

"At least you tried," Caleb said. "You defended your territory. I don't know shit about being a King. I ran."

"You didn't know anything though." Mina comforted him.

"Trajan left, too," Estrella spat. "Fucking deserted us. You should be the leader, Harlow."

"Is everyone forgetting the fact that Trajan is now a hybrid and much more powerful than any of us?" London asked. "You think he's going to let anyone else lead us?"

I let out a sigh. This was ridiculous. We needed to figure out a way to defeat Grayson, and the so-called leader had abandoned his group because he was chasing his woman, yet again.

I wanted Alaric to return, and I could feel myself needing power again. I wasn't used to needing it so often. Was I still sick?

CHAPTER TEN
ALARIC

Ignoring every single plea from Danielle, Alaric trudged through the snow as far away from that fucking house as possible. The wind howled as snow flurried past him in a thick cloud. They all thought he was a killer. Every last one of them. Including Harlow. He didn't know why he was so bothered by that, but he was.

Fucking demons. They were nothing but trouble. He'd find his own way to Grayson and rip that asshole to shreds. He had killed his entire coven. His father. Everyone. Everything he'd ever known, was gone. Anger built inside him like an atomic bomb was about to explode. Alaric's fist connected with a tree, blasting a hole inside it.

"Alaric!" Danielle yelled from behind him. "What are you doing?"

"Get the fuck away from me, Danielle."

Seizing his arm, she turned him around to face her. Her damp dark hair clung to her face. "Talk to me. Did you do something to your blood before you fed it to her?"

"I expect this from Trajan's jealous ass, but from you? He's got you so twisted up in the head with all this bullshit.

You really think this little group of misfits is going to take down Grayson?"

"Yes, I do."

The wind strengthened. He could barely see anything else, but Dani right in front of him. The sight of her used to make him harden in an instant, but now it just angered him. He shouldn't have cared about it anymore.

"Not with Trajan leading. You're so blinded by this, you don't see the bullshit. He's so set on sending me away because the thinks I'm going to steal you that he can't even focus on anything else."

"What? You're so ridiculous. You just want an excuse to leave because you can't stand the fact that I chose him and not you."

That stung a little, but he shrugged it off. "Yeah that's it."

"Then what's your problem, Alaric? Why'd you do that to Harlow?"

"Because I thought I was trying to save her!" he shouted. "Because the thought of her dying scared me." His words surprised him, as well as Danielle by the shocked look in her eyes.

"Then get your fucking head out of your ass and come back. We need you. And she does too."

"You don't need me. And it's clear she believes I tried killing her, too."

"Dani!" Trajan shouted.

"Your ball-and-chain is here." Alaric moved away from her as fast as he could, ignoring her shouts. Unsure of how far he ran, he slowed once he reached what appeared to be a ghost town. It reminded him of the destroyed city he once lived in, and he thought the hybrids probably destroyed this one, too.

He pushed open a door an abandoned building, hoping it wouldn't fall apart. Damn hybrids. He hoped there weren't any dead bodies. Alaric didn't know how he would handle seeing them. He also hoped there wasn't anyone alive. The less people the better. He needed to be alone.

Alaric sat against the wall, holding his head. What the hell had he said to Danielle? He was *scared* of Harlow dying? Why the fuck did he care? She was a fucking demon, who obviously thought he tried to kill her.

Then why did he constantly think about her? Why couldn't he get her out of his head? No matter how much he didn't want to, he cared about her.

Why did she throw up his blood? Was there really something wrong with his blood?

Alaric needed to stop feeling sorry for himself. Since when had he been so damn weak and emotional? He knew he hadn't grieved for anyone because he hadn't had time. He'd seen death often as a vampire, so he was used to it, however, not when it was people he loved and cared about. Maybe that was why he couldn't handle Harlow dying. He couldn't handle another death. But something Danielle had said flashed in his mind. *She needs you.* What had she meant by that? Harlow never acted like she needed him, or anyone for that matter. He was tired of fighting. Fighting with the group. Fighting with himself and his feelings for Harlow. Was it possible that she felt the same strange intense connection as he did?

There was only one way to find out.

CHAPTER ELEVEN
HARLOW

Danielle and Trajan returned hours later, but Alaric wasn't with them. I didn't expect to feel so disappointed, but I was. Not seeing him felt like someone punched me in the stomach. Attempting to appear nonchalant, I casually asked Trajan and Danielle where he was.

"You don't have to worry about him," Trajan said, walking past me. "He's long gone."

My heart dropped, and I swallowed hard. Was he really a spy? Was he really on Grayson's side? He couldn't have been those things. I couldn't believe it.

But why had he run out of there so fast?

"Let it go, Trajan," Danielle said.

"We need to discuss our plan." Trajan ignored her, and everyone convened in the main room. I crossed my arms watching him act like the leader of this group. I had had enough.

"Let's get some things straight," I said, and he snapped his eyes in my direction, clearly appalled. "Are you done chasing after her? Do you think that maybe you could focus on this instead of whatever drama you're creating between her and Alaric?

A muscle twitched in his jaw. "What are you saying?"

"Trajan, we've wasted enough time already on your stupid shit. You and Danielle are together. You have your happy ending. Stop letting it fuck us all up."

I glanced at Danielle and saw her eyebrows raised like she was impressed or something. I didn't care.

"You're pissed at me while that vampire tried to kill you?"

"Jesus, Trajan, he made a mistake."

"Oh, you know this for a fact?"

"Enough!" I shouted. I turned to Danielle. "Let me drink your blood."

"What?"

"I want to try something." I wanted to prove to Trajan that something was wrong with me, and not Alaric.

She went into the kitchen and grabbed a small glass. Her fangs extended, and she bit into her wrist, letting her blood drip into the glass. When she returned to the room, she handed me the glass.

I hesitantly took the glass and drank the blood. Within seconds, I coughed and threw up her blood. Everyone stared in silence, including me. I wasn't sure how I felt. Relieved that Alaric really hadn't tried to kill me but disturbed because something was wrong with me. What was it about vampire blood that was toxic to me?

"What's wrong with you?" Mina asked. "I've drank Caleb's blood many times, and the only thing it did to me was make me stronger and carry some traits of a vampire."

"Nothing is wrong with me," I said, offended. I wasn't diseased, but something had happened to me when Grayson and his hybrids attacked us. I could barely remember that night. Knowing I needed to tell them how weak I had been and how slowly I healed, I didn't. Who knew the two were even related? "Mystery solved. Vampire blood is toxic to me."

"But why?" Trajan asked.

"I don't know. Look, you can't do this anymore." I needed to change the subject. "You're too focused on her and if you're that afraid of losing her, then you can't be leading us. I'm so tired of all of the bullshit with the demons and vampires. The killings. The war. Enough has happened and we need to save our races. We need to focus on killing Grayson and the hybrids."

"Where the hell are we even going to find Grayson?" Alaric asked as he opened the door. I tried ignoring the ridiculous way my heart beat once he appeared. Walking with a sexy, confident gait, with his eyes trained on me, he made his way toward us. "He could be well on his way convincing other vampire covens that demons did this. And with whatever serum he made, god only knows what it'll do to vampires if injected."

"Who said you could return?" Trajan asked, blocking Alaric from moving further into the house.

Danielle seized Trajan's arm, pulling him back. "Enough. He didn't do anything, and we need as many people as we can."

"And we need to act fast," Caleb said. "Enough of the bullshit already."

"I think we need to reach as many vampire covens and demons as we can before Grayson," I told the group. "Convince them to join us to fight him and his hybrids."

Mina rolled her eyes. "Great. So, we're on the great mysterious search for people who may kill us or join us."

"You have a better idea?" Trajan snapped.

"You need to calm down," Caleb said. "Stop talking to her like she's a fucking child."

"Trajan, if you say another word, I swear to god I will force you out of this house," I said, but wondered if I could really force him to do anything since he was now a hybrid.

I hated the way he treated Mina. And everyone else for that matter.

"Will the races need to split up to ask each side?" Mina asked.

"No," I said. "If each group sees that we've teamed up together, it gives more plausibility to our stories. They won't like it at first, but we can convince them."

"Finding more like us is what we're going to have to do," Alaric said. "It's fine. Only way to find out if it works, is if we try. Plus, we do have a card up our sleeve with Trajan being a hybrid. And Caleb being the king of vampires. I will never consider Grayson the king, and after what he's done, I doubt many others will."

Caleb nodded. "Not sure they'll listen to me since I left, but we'll do our best."

"That's all we can do. Let's rest tonight, and tomorrow we'll set out."

"Sounds good," Dmitry said.

"As for Aria and the witches, do we know any witches?" I asked.

"Grayson was talking to some," Trajan said. "Pretty sure they're the ones who came up with the serum to turn demons into hybrids."

Caleb sighed. "Shit, he's got the witches on his side, too?"

"I don't know," Dmitry said. "Aria's friend met a couple. Maybe we could find them and see what they know."

"They threatened to take me," Aria said, her blue eyes widened. "It's Grayson who wants me."

"What would he want with you?" Danielle asked.

"The witches said the new vampire king said I could help them."

Dmitry rubbed the back of his neck and sighed. "We'll figure it out. Let's find Lolly and we can find the witches."

"Why do you think Lolly would ever help us? After what I did?" Aria frowned, and I wondered what had happened.

"You didn't do anything," Dmitry said. "She turned you into the witches. We'll talk to her and convince her of everything. She's human, so we have the advantage of getting inside her head."

"Good idea," I told him. "Is everyone good?"

They agreed, and I made my way to the kitchen needing some alcohol. By some fucked up twist of fate, we were all working together to fight hybrids. It was ridiculous, but if everyone controlled themselves, it could work.

I went to the island, poured a drink, and downed it. A few seconds later, I felt Alaric behind me, and that strange buzz of excitement filled my body. I wanted to feel his arms around me and his lips all over me. I wanted him inside me. Feeling the heat radiating from him, I moved aside.

I cleared my throat. I couldn't be thinking like that. "I'm sorry. For accusing you."

"Mind pouring me one?" His gravelly voice hit me in places I never thought a voice could.

I poured him a drink and watched him swallow it.

"Don't be."

Nodding, I decided to take the bottle with me to my room. The whole day was crazy. Everything in the last seventy-two hours was fucked up. I reached my room and enjoyed the quiet.

Someone knocked on my door and when I opened it, my breath hitched. Alaric stood close. Very close. He held a dangerous look in his emerald eyes.

And I loved it.

"Gonna take the whole bottle and not share?" He flashed a wicked smile, and I could feel my panties soak.

"You're welcome to some. But don't cry if I kick you out early."

He smirked. "I don't cry."

I moved aside, and he walked past me, tall, sexy, and dark. He was a walking sex god. Quiet and mysterious, and as I inhaled his ocean scent, I wanted to devour him.

"Are you okay?" Alaric crossed his muscular arms in front of his chest. Wearing a simple T-shirt and jeans made him look sexier.

"I'm fine." I closed the door.

"Should I go?"

"No. I like your company. Surprisingly. It shocks me."

"What does? This?" he asked, motioning our conversation.

"Yeah. Being in the same room as a vampire is a little strange for me."

"Tell me about it. Never thought I'd be this close proximity with a demon and not want to kill them."

"That makes one of us."

A bitter smile curved his lips, but his eyes devoured me. "You don't want to kill me."

"I'm sure if I tried, I'd have a group of them after me."

"Then I guess you and I are at an impasse."

I closed the distance between us. My heart beating like a drum. Wanting to feel his touch again. "I guess we are. What are we gonna do about it?"

Staring into my eyes with lust, I knew he wanted me, but he snatched the bottle from my hands and poured himself a drink by the window. It felt as if he had poured ice all over me. But I knew why he did it. I was a demon. And demons and vampires didn't mix.

We sat in my room drinking in silence for a few minutes, me sitting on the bed, and Alaric sitting beside the window in the moonlight.

"Do you really believe we can all work together?" he asked.

"I don't know." I moved toward him, holding out my glass. We stood there, staring at each other. I didn't understand what was happening, but my entire body hummed with a fire I had never felt before. Every part of me throbbed.

He poured some whiskey in my glass.

"Do you?"

Alaric downed another drink, and his eyes stared at me like a man with a deep desire. It was strange. No man had ever looked at me the way he did. He hated demons though. I hated vampires. And didn't he think the worst of me? I needed to apologize to him. What had Danielle said to him for him to return.

"Might as well. It's going to be hard convincing the vampires since they're following Grayson. They hate demons. However, a lot of the elders died. Including my father. I don't know why they attacked their own kind."

"I'm sorry." What the fuck was wrong with me? Why did I keep apologizing to him? I didn't care.

"I'm sorry for your losses, too. I knew Grayson was up to something. And he's got the witches involved."

"How is he convincing all breeds to do what he wants? It makes no sense. What is he promising them?"

Alaric shook his head. "I have no idea."

"Think we could get the witches to be on our side?"

"Maybe, but I've never had much luck with witches. They hate vampires, which makes this whole situation even stranger."

"Well, maybe Dmitry and Aria can convince her friend—"

"Her friend tried to out her, unknowingly. What I don't understand is what the witches, or Grayson, want with Aria. She's a human. Or was."

I sighed and collapsed on the bed. "I never thought in a million years I'd be sharing whiskey with a vampire in my room."

"Ditto. Roles reversed."

"Why'd you come back?"

He cleared his throat. "I shouldn't have left."

"Guess Danielle's pretty convincing."

"She can be."

I hated the jealous feeling rising inside me. It was ridiculous. "It isn't just your blood that makes me sick. I tried Danielle's blood. Same reaction."

"What happened to you?"

"Nothing. Maybe I'm a rare demon breed who can't handle vampire blood."

"You're rare indeed." Meeting his eyes, I tried reading his expression, but he was good at hiding. I understood. I did the same thing.

"How'd you become a vampire?" I asked, hoping to shift the conversation away from the tension.

"Vampires ravaged a village. We were only peasants who didn't have anything. What about you?"

"I was raised by demons. My parents were killed by vampires. They turned me when I was seventeen."

"Fuck."

We had finished the bottle, but neither one of us made a move to leave or force the other out. I was mesmerized by how the moonlight illuminated Alaric's face. I could see pain in his eyes and I wanted to take it away. I didn't understand what was wrong with me. These thoughts never crossed my mind. He was beautiful, and I couldn't stop staring.

When he turned his head, I immediately looked away, but as I returned my gaze, his eyes were locked on me. The heat in the room made my body pulsate again. He looked at me like he wanted to fuck me silly, but there was more to his gaze that I couldn't detect.

He set his glass down and stood, sauntering toward me. My heart pounded, but I didn't move. I only watched in anticipation for what he would do. He stopped right at the edge of the bed and slowly climbed on top of me.

"This is so wrong," he whispered against my neck.

I moaned, wanting more, not caring how wrong it was. I felt his hard cock pressing against me, and my insides were exploding with desire. "We can't do this."

"I know."

I pushed his chest slightly. "You should go."

He nodded, removing his warm body from me. "Yeah. I'll…I'll see you in the morning." He left the room and I let out a long breath.

I hated being alone. I wished he hadn't left, even if he was a vampire, but he made me feel, *different*. He didn't make me feel like a monster. He made me feel like I mattered and that I was worthy. Was that his charm? Or was it real? I was tired of fighting against it. I wanted to give in to the feelings. Explore them. Let them take over.

I shook my head. I was getting well ahead of myself and I needed to rest if we were going on some witch hunt tomorrow.

CHAPTER TWELVE
ALARIC

Alaric returned to his room feeling completely high, yet disappointed. What had that woman done to him? He couldn't stop thinking about her. He wanted her, and he hated that she wanted him to leave. Couldn't they have their own affair? Everyone else in the house was. Why couldn't they? Maybe she didn't feel the same way toward him. Maybe it was all just sex to her.

But she didn't act that way. He saw the desire in her eyes. Her body language. Could he be so wrong about something?

The door to his room opened, and that sexy demon slithered inside, wearing a simple white gown that just covered her enough. She closed the door.

"Change your mind?" he asked.

"Shut the fuck up," she said, and kissed him so hard, he thought she was going to make his lips fall off. Everything inside him burst into a fiery explosion. He lifted her, pressing her against the wall as her legs wrapped around him. She quickly unbuttoned his pants and guided his hard cock inside her warmth.

"Oh fuck." She tightened around his dick, squeezing him. It was amazing. Her greedy pussy seemed to latch onto his cock and he wanted to give her all he had. He rocked into her, hard, as she dug her nails into his back.

"Harder, you pussy."

Alaric clenched his teeth and slammed into her hard. She wanted it rough, he'd give her rough. He carried her to the bed, dropping her. Ripping off her gown, he wrestled her to her stomach, and shoved his cock inside her dripping wet pussy. She cried out as he lifted her ass in the air and dove deeper. Grabbing her hair, he smacked her ass twice.

"Is that all you've got?"

He seized her tit, squeezing it hard, then he slapped it. "You'd better behave, filthy girl."

"Or what?" She twisted her head, staring back at him with a challenge in her ruby eyes. "Are you going to fuck me like a man finally?"

He thrust into her, slapping her ass, hard, wishing he had a whip or something. He definitely needed a gag to shut her up. He spit on her backside, letting it slide down near her nether region. Slipping a finger into her ass, she moaned, pushing back against him, eager for more.

She rose up, her back rubbing against his chest. Seizing her throat, with his other hand he reached around to her clit, pinching and pulling it. He slapped it and she shuddered, holding onto the back of his neck. He watched her tits bounce as he rocked inside her, slapping her clit, again and again. Her moans were loud, and he longed to see those red eyes. Having her neck next to his mouth, he inhaled her sweet scent. His fangs extended, and he wasn't sure he could hold back any longer.

Alaric wanted to claim her, but he wasn't sure he could. "I want to bite you. Claim you, Harlow."

"Do it."

Without hesitation, he sank his teeth into her neck, tasting her sweet blood. She cried out as he felt her sex soak his dick.

Harlow got back on all fours, completely at his mercy. "Fuck me, Alaric. Do what you want to me." She purred.

He impaled his rock-hard cock inside her and she growled. Reaching for her clit, he slapped it, and vigorously rubbed it as he fucked her hard, like a man. He could feel an intense connection between them. He couldn't wait to tie her up some day and really have his way with her.

Harlow gripped the sheets. "Oh fuck, yes," she cried out as her pussy tightened around his cock. He knew she was coming, so he picked up his pace. Goddamn she felt amazing. He licked her neck where he'd bitten her, healing it, and thrust into her until he felt the tingles over his body. When he pulled out of her, he felt a strange emptiness. They both collapsed on the bed.

"Goddamn," she said, breathless. "Who knew a vampire could fuck so hard?"

"Who knew a demon could be fucked so hard?"

He looked at her naked body, admiring each curvature. She was fucking hot. Sex with her was intense, more than any other woman he'd been with before. It made him weak in the knees thinking about how tight and wet she was. And listening to her moans drove him over the edge.

He stilled.

Alaric bit her. A demon. He had bitten a demon. But Harlow wasn't a demon. She was more than that. She was fierce and loyal. Sexy and strong.

What was he thinking? Apparently, only thinking with his dick. What was going through her mind?

Goddamn. What had he gotten himself into?

"I could fuck you all night," he said.

"We can't keep doing this."

"I know." He knew it, but he didn't want to give her up. She made him feel amazing, and she challenged him. He rolled onto his back, letting the moon bathe him in its light.

"This was fun, though," she said and dressed. "I needed the power. Sleep well."

Alaric sat up. "Are you fucking serious?"

Harlow reached the door and turned back. "What?"

He stood, towering over her. "That's all this is to you? Just some fuck so you can get your power?"

"What do you want it to be?"

"I don't know, Harlow. For whatever reason, I'm just letting the feelings take over." Why was it so difficult to talk to her? Tell her exactly what he was feeling? How could he, when he didn't know himself?

"I don't fall in love, Alaric. I never have, and I never will."

He shook his head. "Took the words right out of my mouth."

"Then we're done here, right?"

He wanted to fuck her again. He had just fucking bit her, claiming her, and now she was running away. If that was what she wanted, so be it. "You really are a demon. Selfish and uncouth. You feel nothing."

She clenched her teeth and breathed hard. "What do you expect from me? You want me to be your rebound because losing Danielle is too hard for you?"

"Fuck you. This has nothing to do with her and you know it." Was that all she felt from him? They hadn't known each other long, and it hadn't been very smooth, but there was something between them. Or so he thought.

"Whatever. That's all I am to you, and all you are is a good fuck." She left the room taking all the warmth, leaving him lonely.

CHAPTER THIRTEEN
HARLOW

What a dick!

How could Alaric think *I* was the selfish one? He clearly only wants to make Danielle jealous, and by the way she took off after him earlier, he succeeded in that. How could he believe that I felt nothing?

I sank down onto my bed knowing exactly how he felt that way. But demons and vampires couldn't be together. I kept telling myself that and I was tired of hearing it. Tired of telling myself that.

I touched my neck where Alaric had bitten me. Claimed me. I wasn't exactly sure what that meant, but I didn't think vampires claimed just anyone. Did Alaric really have feelings for me? Were we just two stubborn mules dancing around each other, afraid to let anything good happen? I couldn't stop how I felt about him, and no matter what, I knew those thoughts and feelings, whatever they were, wouldn't vanish overnight. Especially after the night we had just spent.

The way he made me feel like I was the only one who mattered to him wasn't lost on me. But maybe it was for the best that we avoided each other. All we had done was fight and fuck and accuse each other.

The sliver of orange light caught my eye, and as I looked out the window at the rising sun, I gripped the edge of my bed, wishing Alaric were there with me. Maybe he was just a good fuck. But I'd had good fucks before, not like him though, and I never thought twice about them.

My body ached, and I had no idea why I wasn't healing like I should've been. Was having sex with a vampire weakening me? Mina and Trajan weren't weakened. Maybe I needed to swallow my ego and talk to Alaric. Tell him that he wasn't a good fuck.

But what was he to me? What did I want? I wasn't lying when I said I didn't fall in love. Love was a foreign concept to me. It never existed.

CHAPTER FOURTEEN
ALARIC

Waking up from the sun's light was something Alaric loved, but he missed its warmth. At least he was able to see it. He wished he had his arms around Harlow, kissing her neck and being inside of her.

Fuck.

He had to stop thinking about her. Nothing would ever happen between them again. Especially since all he was to her was a good fuck. Why did that matter? If the sex was that good, they could at least continue that.

When he got out of the bed, there was a quick knock and the door opened. Harlow walked in, looked down, and gasped, but tried hiding it.

Alaric smirked, loving the way she stared at him. "It's okay to look. You seemed to really have enjoyed it last night."

Harlow let out a disgusted sigh. "You wish. You were...mediocre."

"Ouch." He moved closer toward her. "You didn't like it? Do I need to try again? You need more strength?" The closer he got to her, the more she backed away until her back hit the door.

"No. I have an excellent memory."

"So, do I." He leaned down to her ear. "And from the amazing sounds you made last night, I think you liked it more than you lead on." Alaric could hear her racing heartbeat as his hands moved to her hips. Leaning down, he pressed his lips to hers, and she responded by wrapping her hands around his head. Harlow pulled him close and his cock hardened. The passionate way she kissed him made him want her even more, which was ridiculous. He shouldn't have been falling for another woman if she was only going to break his heart. But they were just having fun, right?

He reached to touch her breast, but the thoughts kept invading his mind, distracting him. He pulled away and rested his forehead against hers.

"We shouldn't do this," he whispered. "It's bad. You said so yourself."

"It doesn't have to be." She met his eyes.

He sighed. He wanted to press her for information, but why was he so insistent? Why was he being such a goddamn pussy? "Just tell me what this is."

"I…" Her body swayed a little and she lost her balance, but he caught her.

"Are you okay?"

"I-I'm fine." She rubbed her temples. "I need more energy."

"I'll get dressed and we'll go."

"You can't. The sun's out and we need to talk to the group about who's doing what."

"That'll take two seconds. Unless everyone's going to start bitching or causing drama."

Harlow smirked, and it lifted a little darkness. "And how are you going to get away from the sun?"

"It will set in twenty minutes."

Alaric threw on some clothes, and together they made their way down to the main room. Mina, Caleb, Sawyer, Dmitry, and Aria were in the kitchen drinking coffee. Dmitry offered some to Alaric and Harlow, who was now looking pale.

"Thanks," Alaric said, taking a cup. "Look, she needs to feed. Do you know when Danielle and Trajan and the rest are coming down?"

"Not a clue," Dmitry said, and turned to Mina. "I think you and Caleb should go with Danielle and Trajan. Caleb needs to regain his power as the vampire king. Sawyer, you, Estrella, and London seek out more demons. The rest of us should join forces and find these witches."

Mina frowned. "I don't like that."

"I know, but you and Caleb can handle those two. It's clear some of us can't work together."

Harlow rolled her eyes, but then closed them like she had a headache.

"What's wrong, Harlow?" Dmitry asked.

"I just need energy."

Had demons lost energy that quickly? Alaric didn't think so, and by the confused look on Dmitry's face, it wasn't normal. Something had happened to her. But what? Was she hiding something?

"We'll find demons," Sawyer said. "But I need to find Caroline, too."

Caleb raised an eyebrow. "That's very risky."

"You'd do the same if it were Mina."

No one disagreed with him.

"Come on. Let's go." Dmitry took Aria's hand.

Mina rushed to hug him. "Good luck. And please be careful."

"Always."

Alaric wanted to take Harlow's hand, but instead he placed his hand at the small of her back in case she would fall. He didn't know what was wrong with her, but he hoped they'd find out soon. He knew they needed to talk about them, but Harlow needed to get well first.

CHAPTER FIFTEEN
HARLOW

The wind was unforgiving and no matter how much I tried to keep myself warm, it was like all heat escaped me. I didn't know how Aria was able to handle it, but since she was part demon now or whatever the fuck, if that was even possible, I guessed she could bear it.

Feeling Alaric's hand on my back helped, but I wanted more. I hated feeling that way, but I did. We needed to talk, but what was the point? We were about to go to war. Would he still want me when it was over? What if Trajan died, would he wind up with Danielle? Why was I feeling so many emotions lately?

I shook my head. It was the sickness.

Once we reached a populated area, we looked for the perfect victim. I enjoyed searching for my victims instead of being given a name from the Dominus. It had always cheated me out of the true hunt. I wanted to see someone in the act of doing evil so that I could rip their head off or squeeze their heart until the last beat. But as I watched people walk by us, I couldn't see the evil. I saw colorful lighted displays and trees decorated with lights. It was the humans' holiday. Something demons didn't celebrate or understand. I always hated that time because the amount of evil seemed scarce.

"Should I grab a victim?" Alaric asked.

"They're all innocent."

"No one's truly innocent."

I met his green eyes. He was right. No one was truly innocent, but no one deserved to die without reason.

"I think I can find some for you," Aria spoke. I almost forgot she was there. We all turned to her. "Um, yeah, so my friend, or whatever, used to hang out in this bar with a lot of shady people."

"Looks like we can kill two birds with one stone," Dmitry said.

"How far away is it? Harlow needs to feed. We'll just go find someone and meet you back here."

When I looked up at him, I wondered why he was focusing on me so much. Was he trying to lure me away from the group to kill me?

Dmitry nodded. "Okay."

Alaric took my hand, and we blended into the crowd of people shopping or dining. He grabbed a man, pulling him deep into an alley. He compelled the man to cooperate, and Alaric sank his fangs into his neck. His eyes were black as the night sky above and sexy. Watching him choose a random person mesmerized me. He didn't know the man's backstory. Didn't know if the man was good or not. His need to feed overpowered any of those notions. He hunted for his food. He wasn't given food like a snake in a cage waiting for the rat to fall.

Once I saw the man's life energy begin to escape, I rushed over and ingested it, letting it fill me. Its warmth overcame me, and I relished the familiar feeling. My body tingled with electricity, and as Alaric's eyes turned from black to green, I wanted him. As if he read my mind, he rushed up to me, his lips meeting mine in a hot kiss. He unbuttoned my pants, slid them down, and lifted me. My legs wrapped around him as my body throbbed with an intense need for him. He kissed me like he couldn't get enough of me. Alaric released his hard cock and plunged it inside my wet heat, filling me completely.

"I want to do bad things to you, Harlow, but this has to be quick this time."

"Fuck me, Alaric."

He slammed into me hard. Bits of the brick wall fell to the ground. Heat poured over me and I felt satisfied. I wanted it to be longer, he was right. It had to be quick. Pumping into me once, twice, three times, he emptied his seed inside me.

"You feel amazing," he said, pulling out of me.

"So, do you." There was an intense connection between us, but it couldn't be more than that. He was just a good fuck. I wouldn't let him complete me. I couldn't. It would only end badly.

Feeling even more powerful, I was ready to face witches.

We dressed and met Aria and Dmitry a few minutes later. The snow began to fall as we made our way toward the witches, away from the town of happy, holiday shoppers. We trudged deeper into the dark forest.

"You think Lolly is still around there?" Dmitry asked. "Or did she join the witches?"

Aria shrugged. "I don't know. She really liked them, but who knows if it's even real. They were probably just using her to get to me."

"What do these witches want with you?" Alaric asked.

"I don't know. They didn't say much."

"We need to find your friend."

"We will," Alaric said as we started walking again.

Dizziness consumed me. I hated feeling that way, and I didn't know what it was. Was I turning into a human? What happened during that fight with the hybrids? Had they injected me with something? All I remembered was the bomb that went off and nothing else. Grayson had the witches create a serum to turn demons into hybrids. What if he had injected me after I passed out? But if I were turning into a hybrid, I wouldn't be sick and weak.

We trekked for several more miles, but I wasn't sure how much longer I could go. My body was weakening again. I didn't understand what was happening. I fed, and I had sex. I shouldn't have been weak. I was panting and couldn't catch my breath. My knees gave out on me and I collapsed in the snow.

"Harlow are you okay?" Alaric asked in a worried voice. "Let me carry you." He came up behind me, and as much as I loved his voice and wanted him, I wanted to get better. I didn't want to be a weakling. Demons weren't weak. I hated that a vampire was helping me, acknowledging my weakness. He'd already carried me before. The last thing I needed was a vampire pretending to care, when I knew damn well all they wanted was to kill demons. They wanted to torture us. He had already tried to kill me.

"No!" I shouted. "I'm not a fucking weak woman to you. I'm a goddamn demon. I don't need your help."

He backed away. "You need help."

"Don't tell me what I need." Everyone stared at me, and I wanted to stand and keep moving, but I couldn't budge.

"Jesus, I'm not going to do anything."

"Harlow, we need to keep moving," Dmitry said. "Let him carry you."

Anger welled inside me and I knew my eyes were red because Aria hid behind Dmitry with wide eyes.

"I can do this. You think he wants to help me? He tried to kill me."

"Are you fucking serious right now?" Alaric snapped.

"Get away from me."

Alaric clenched his teeth and began walking away. Aria's eyes followed him and after exchanging a look with Dmitry, she chased after him.

Dmitry kneeled next to me. "What was that all about?"

"I don't need a fucking vampire coming to my rescue every five minutes. I'm not a damsel in distress."

He sighed. His long hair was wet and frizzy from the snow, but he still looked hot. "Harlow, he's not out to get any of us. No matter what Trajan tried to implant in your head."

"Dmitry, you don't get it. I can't fall for a vampire. I can't let him take care of me. No vampire has ever shown me that kindness, and just because he's the first one doesn't mean he actually cares. He could have something up his sleeve. They're so manipulative. How do we know he isn't part of Grayson?"

He shook his head. "Why are you so paranoid? We already proved that Alaric is innocent. Did Trajan say something to you?"

"Nothing that wasn't true."

"Look, I don't know the guy that well, but he's really into you. Not many men look at women the way he looks at you."

"Dmitry, I just need to feed right now, okay?"

"Why are you running out of energy so fast?" he asked, pulling me to my feet.

"I don't know."

My eyes were closing, and my legs refused to work. It was happening again. I was going to black out. My pulse quickened, and I couldn't breathe. Collapsing against Dmitry's chest, I closed my eyes.

CHAPTER SIXTEEN
ALARIC

"Alaric," Aria called.

"You're very brave to be chasing a pissed off vampire."

"I know, but I know you won't hurt me. Plus, I'm stronger than you think I am."

He twisted around and was face to face with the blonde beauty. Her soft blue eyes stared at him with an innocence, yet he saw her fierce determination as well. He heard the pounding of her heart, and once he saw the veins in her neck pulsate, he wondered how sweet her blood would taste. But she was right. He'd never hurt her. She was becoming a demon, and the more she gave into the demon, the less human she would be.

"I'm not running away, if that's what you're worried about. I just needed a moment."

"No that isn't what I'm worried about, but you can't keep running away. I used to be a runner, and it doesn't do anything but make it worse. Harlow isn't herself."

"Clearly. She just fed, but her body is rejecting everything. But what she said, she meant."

"No, she didn't. I think she's right about the witches."

"Is there something you know?"

"We know the witches are working with Grayson. What if they were there when they attacked the Lair? They can make themselves invisible to people. They can make anyone see what they want them to see. What if they injected her with something?"

He thought about it. There was no way they would've known witches were involved because they hid their scent. The only way he could tell a person was a witch was if he touched them. "Why just her? There were several demons there."

"Maybe it was random. I mean, some of the demons died."

"What would they inject her with? Not the hybrid serum."

"No. The witches want me. When Grayson learned about me, maybe he wanted to turn Dmitry into a hybrid in order to get me to come to Grayson. But when Trajan showed up in the Underground, he took advantage. Demons always stick up for each other and are always a tight knit group. Turning Trajan into a hybrid would surely lure us to him, especially since he is a Dominus member. Maybe getting another Dominus member would force the demons to turn me in."

"None of that makes any sense. If all they want is you, they wouldn't go through so much trouble. They wouldn't just injure us or turn us into the most powerful breed. They'd kill us if we stood in the way of something they're trying to accomplish."

"Well, they're helping Grayson kill demons and vampires for not becoming hybrids. If they create enough chaos, the demons who refuse to become hybrids and who survive will be forced to turn me in to the witches, because maybe turning me in will end the war."

"But why does Grayson or the witches want you?"

"We're going to find Lolly to see if she can set us up with the witches."

Alaric shook his head. "We're basically handing you over, you realize that."

"If it wasn't for me, maybe none of this would have happened."

"What are you talking about? Grayson was up to no good before anyone even heard about you."

"But I made it worse. Somehow."

"You didn't, Aria. I assure you that. Fucking witches can play with us. We aren't exactly on good terms with them."

"It's okay. Dmitry has a plan. We find Lolly and remove her from the witches and try to get answers out of her."

"That's the plan? You expect us to kidnap some human from witches and torture answers out of her?"

"We're going to the bar she frequents, but we aren't going to torture her."

"How are we even going to get close to her?"

"I'm going to try my best to talk to her before she can warn them. It's our only choice. And for what it's worth, I know Harlow didn't mean those things she said. She's sick and defensive. She's not used to being that way. I used to be weak all of the time and I let someone take advantage of that, but now I'm stronger, and I refuse to be that weak again. I refuse to let someone use that against me."

"I was trying to help her. I wasn't going to take advantage of it."

"I know, and she knows that, too. But she acts like she may have been in a similar situation as me, so it could just take time."

Alaric crossed his arms in front of his chest. "Why are you saying all of this?"

"Because I know how hard it is to want to help someone you love who doesn't want help. I know she cares about you. And I see the pain in both of your eyes, but today, it was gone. You help each other. Maybe I'm a sucker for a happy ending, too."

He had no words, and he didn't know what to say.

Alaric stiffened once he heard someone trudging in the snow. He turned around and saw Dmitry carrying Harlow in his arms, unconscious. His heart dropped as he rushed to her, brushing aside her hair.

"She needs help, fast."

"Where is this bar?" he asked Aria.

"It's across from the Black River. It's called Echo."

Alaric took Harlow into his arms. "I'll meet you there."

"Wait!" Dmitry shouted after him, but he was too fast, and he refused to stop. He was faster than demons, and he knew with Aria still in transition, she wouldn't be able to keep up. He hated splitting up from them, but he had no choice.

Alaric shot through the forest, the trees speeding past. He knew he should've spared his energy, but he didn't care. Harlow needed help and he didn't care if she hated him when she woke up. He was going to save her, whether it killed him or not.

CHAPTER SEVENTEEN
ALARIC

A small city came into view, and Alaric zeroed in on sounds from a bar. Frantically searching for Echo, he turned down a street with one lone bar. Music, people drunkenly talking and laughing echoed into the street. Some argued. Pool balls clacked, and glasses clinked and broke. Alaric had no idea how there would be people inside this bar who would help a vampire and a demon.

When Alaric opened the door, he felt the stares of several people all at once. Everyone had stopped in their tracks, and some heavy metal song blared from the speakers. He didn't know who he needed to find.

"I need help," he shouted over the music.

A man with long brown hair greeted him. "And you think this is the place to bring your kind?"

"Look, I know what this looks like—"

"Yeah, it looks like a vampire is bringing in a dead demon to a witch bar. We don't want anything to do with your kind."

"I'm not here to start anything."

"That's what the last vampire said."

"What vampire?"

"The King of vampires, as he calls himself."

"Grayson was here? I thought you were all working with him."

A cluster of witches crept closer to Alaric, but he held his ground. He was getting pissed and tried holding back his anger, but he knew if they wanted to harm him they could easily. "Again, I'm not here for any trouble. She needs help. Please."

"And you have come to the wrong place."

"I'm not with Grayson!" he yelled.

"You're a vampire. You're all with him, and we are tired of doing his bidding."

"No. I'm friends with Aria and she's on her way here."

"Aria, the human?" the man questioned, and his expression softened to curiosity.

"Yes."

"Give her to me," a woman with dark wavy hair walked up to Alaric, in a soft voice. Her hazel eyes roved across Harlow. "We will take care of her."

"Do you know what's wrong with her?"

"No, but I can find out."

"Just tell me where to take her," he said. He didn't trust any of them, especially since they decided to help at the first mention of Aria. What was it about Aria that everyone wanted? And if the witches were on Grayson's side, why the strong reaction toward Grayson?

As he followed the woman, he passed by twins with the same dark hair and blue eyes and a human with curly auburn hair who stared at him. He wondered if that was Aria's friend, Lolly. He couldn't read her mind though, a trick the witches used.

The woman led him up the wooden stairs to a hallway full of rooms. She opened the door to a basic room. A bed rested against the wall in the corner and there was a table underneath a window with a couple of chairs. He carefully lay Harlow down on the bed, and when she moaned, his pulse quickened.

"Is she going to be okay…?" he asked, hoping for a name.

"Gemma."

"Alaric."

"I don't know if she's going to be okay. What happened to her?"

"Grayson's hybrids attacked, and we fought them. Next thing I know, she's sick. She can't keep her strength."

Gemma removed part of Harlow's collar and sighed. "She's been bitten."

Alaric cleared his throat. "I bit her. But that's never been an issue. I know a few mixed couples and they've been fine."

She pressed her lips in a thin line and shook her head. How much of this world had he not known? He'd been around for centuries, but he'd never cared to learn much about demons.

"Demons and vampires cannot mix."

"We seem to do just fine."

"Demons who are bitten by vampires end up dying."

"What? That's not even remotely true."

"I'm a witch who has seen more than you can even imagine. Why would you even want to save her? She's a demon. Don't demons and vampires torture each other?"

"Some do. My biting her is not what's making her sick. She was sick before that."

Gemma sighed again and placed her hands onto Harlow's chest. Harlow's skin glowed and Alaric saw her veins pumping with blood. Scars became prominent on her shoulder and he wondered if they were from the battle. Harlow was strong, and she had to make it out alive. She deserved that much.

"She's been poisoned," Gemma said finally.

"Poisoned? With what?"

"A potion."

"What kind of potion?" he asked, becoming impatient. Why did witches always take their time explaining things?

Gemma stood from Harlow's bed and moved toward the door, but something about her timid demeanor put Alaric on edge.

"What is it?"

"I need ingredients to create an antidote. I'll be back." She slipped out the door faster than Alaric could ask questions. Something was up, and he felt uneasy putting his and Harlow's lives in the hands of witches. He didn't want to be in a place full of witches with Harlow in her condition, but he had no choice. He sat on the edge of the bed and ran his hand through her soft blonde hair. He could barely hear her heartbeat, and her skin had paled even more.

Fuck.

She needed help, and she needed it fast. Who had poisoned her? Why would they do that to her?

Aria had guessed the witches were at the Lair at the time of the attack, and she was right. But it still didn't make sense that Harlow was the only one affected. Or was she? Were there other demons who had died from the poison? He hated mentioning Aria to the witches, but he had to. He knew they wouldn't have helped him. He needed to warn Dmitry and Aria from coming, but he wasn't going to leave Harlow.

Gemma returned with a handful of bottles and herbs. "When I inject this into her, it will take days for her to heal."

"Days?"

"Yes. Just make yourself comfortable."

"Sure. A vampire stuck in a house full of witches. It'll be like a vacation."

She smirked and set the ingredients down on the table. She began to mix them together like it was something she had done a million times. If Alaric wasn't so worried for Harlow, he may have actually paid attention to whatever Gemma threw together so he'd be able to create the concoction next time someone got sick. Unless there would never be a next time since they'd all be dead by the witches' hands.

Once Gemma finished, she shook the brown liquid, said a little spell, and grabbed a syringe. She pushed the liquid into Harlow's veins and it seemed to glow throughout Harlow. Alaric had never seen anything like it.

"She'll be asleep through the night. You should get some rest." Gemma reached the door and turned back around. "When did you say Aria was coming?"

"Why are you so concerned with her arrival? Have you all been expecting us?"

"No, of course not."

"What do the witches want with Aria?"

"I-I do not know."

"How did she get poisoned?"

"I don't know that either."

Alaric slammed his hand down on the table, making her jump. "Do you know anything? Does anyone down there know anything?"

"I-I will ask. Good night." She opened the door, slipped out, and closed it fast. She wasn't going to run away from him though. He opened the door, and as he took a step, he slammed into an invisible wall. He couldn't escape, and then it dawned on him. Gemma cast a spell on the room, barricading them inside. Were they that afraid of vampires and demons? Keeping them in a locked room to make sure they didn't kill the precious witches. He wanted to yell and scream, but Harlow needed to rest. He swore the next time he saw a witch come into the room he would get answers. If not, they'd be his next victim.

Alaric took a deep breath, trying to calm his nerves. Were they holding them hostage in case Aria didn't show? Running his hands through his hair, he settled in the chair near the window. He usually looked out the window, but instead, he watched Harlow's chest move up and down in a beautiful rhythmic way. He eagerly waited for her to wake. He couldn't wait to see those brown eyes that turned red.

Shaking his head, he didn't understand what this woman had done to him, but she had transfixed him like some spell. Was that what the witches did? Made her weak so that the two of them would fall in love?

There was a soft knock at the door, and a few seconds later, the human with curly auburn hair entered. Fear shown in her brown eyes, but she tried to appear brave. Alaric could hear her pounding heartbeat.

"What do you want?"

"I came to check on your friend."

"She's asleep. But if she ends up dead, you're all going to have a very pissed off vampire on your hands."

"You're one vampire among a group of witches."

"They sent the human in here?"

"No, I came on my own."

"Either you're incredibly naïve, or stupid."

"You don't scare me."

"Your heartbeat says otherwise." And he could read her mind all of a sudden. A thousand thoughts crowded inside. She was scared but intrigued. She wanted to know more about him, as vampires had always been a fascinating idea to her. Vampires were part of her dark desire.

She swallowed hard. "Aria told you about this place, didn't she?"

"You brought the witches to the Downward Spiral. They figured out where the Lair was, didn't they?"

"Demons and vampires shouldn't exist."

Alaric couldn't help but smirk. She wasn't under any protection cloak for whatever reason, and he could smell her blood. The sweet scent strengthened the faster her heart beat. He ambled toward her. With every inch that diminished between them, the harder her heart pounded. "We shouldn't exist, but we do. And somewhere deep down inside you love that we do exist. Sure, witches can be fun." Her brown eyes exposed her lust. Clearly, she wanted him. "But you know vampires and demons are more fun. We can make your wildest dreams come true."

She gasped.

He moved behind her, brushing her curls from her neck, and she moaned. She eagerly offered herself and he smiled, letting his fangs extend. He was seconds from tasting her sweet blood. Inches from her neck, he said, "you want me?"

"Yes." She panted. He could smell her arousal.

Alaric faced her, and stared into her eyes to compel her, but the door swung open and he sprinted to the window as if nothing had happened.

"What are you doing in here, Lolly," a man asked in a British accent. He was one of the twins Alaric saw earlier, the one gripping Lolly like she was his property. His boyish looks made him seem like he was fifteen. He was tall and fit, and like the rest of the witches, gave off no indication as to what they were, almost as if their scent was hidden.

"I-I don't know. I was checking on them."

"You stupid girl. How many times do I have to tell you it's too dangerous?"

"You think I'm really going to hurt her?" Alaric asked, crossing his arms in front of his chest.

"You're a vampire."

"I am. But I'm not so dumb as to kill the only normal human in this joint, especially when you're helping my friend."

"Just a cautionary thing. I'm Ezekiel, but you can call me Zeke." He held out his hand, but Alaric knew better than to touch a witch's hand.

"Alaric. That's Harlow."

Zeke removed his hand and gave a sly smile as he placed his arm around Lolly. He was cloaking her. "Friends with Aria, I hear. She's the one who attacked Lolly. She distinctly remembers her eyes turning a ruby red during the attack."

"I was unaware of that."

"She's a demon, now. We're hopeful that she's still useful to us."

"What do you want with her? Doesn't Grayson want her? She said you and your brother came to the Lair looking for her."

"We don't work with Grayson. But he thinks we do. We're only trying to protect Aria, since your kind is keenly interested in her. At first, we intended to bring her to the vampires, but we have better plans for her."

"Which are?"

"All will be revealed in due time. For now, I need to go teach my girl, Lolly, a couple of lessons." He pulled her close to his body as he opened the door.

"Who poisoned Harlow?"

Zeke turned to face him and shrugged. "Oh, one more thing. I spelled the window so that when the sun comes up, it won't burn you."

"Thanks," Alaric told him, but it felt all wrong.

"Don't thank me yet." Zeke closed the door after them, and Alaric sighed. Something was up, and he didn't like their hospitality. He didn't like the way Zeke held onto Lolly and treated her in general. Was she being used by the witches and was unaware? She seemed desperate to belong in a world like that.

What price would he and Harlow have to pay for them saving her?

CHAPTER EIGHTEEN
HARLOW

Murmured voices pulled me from a deep sleep. My body was exhausted, and opening my eyes was difficult since it felt like my eyelids had been glued shut. When my vision finally came to focus, I saw a beautiful man sitting by the window, and tried remembering where we were. The room looked unfamiliar. I felt weak. The weakness reminded me of vampires locking me up and torturing me for months.

The man turned toward me. It was Alaric and I gasped.

"You're awake," he said and kneeled beside me.

I jerked away from him, my back hitting the wall. "Where am I?"

"We're in…a witch bar."

"A what?"

"Yeah. You passed out and I had to get you help."

"Help? You fucking asshole. What did these witches do to me?"

"They saved you. Trust me, I didn't want to trust them, and I still don't. But you're alive."

"What are you doing to me? Why are you torturing me?" I jerked the covers off me and jumped toward the door. I had to get out of there, but when I turned the knob, the door didn't open. I tried and tried, but nothing happened. "What is this?" I faced him, gripping the doorknob.

"The witches locked us in here." His calm demeanor annoyed me.

"What kind of sick game is this? Why are you doing this? Why are you so calm?"

"Harlow, I'm not doing anything. The witches are keeping us in here."

"Why? Are you in on this?"

"Jesus, what is your problem? Is this paranoia part of your sickness? Why do you always assume I'm out to get you? I know vampires and demons don't exactly have the best relationships, but fuck. Do you know what you do to me?"

"I repulse you. All vampires hate demons. All they do is torture us."

"Torture you? You gotta be fucking kidding me. Demons are the ones who tortured us."

He was delusional. "Don't patronize me. We aren't the ones who were made by your kind and then were used as fucking science experiments."

Alaric quickly removed his shirt, and I gasped. It was the first time I'd seen him in the light. The clean lines on his chest made my heart skip, but it was the long, deep scars across his chest and stomach that my heart drop. "These were caused by demons. I was tortured for years. You think demons have always been innocent? Why do you think I hate demons so much? You're not exactly a perfect breed."

"What?" It was too much for me to handle. Demons didn't torment vampires. That wasn't who we were. He had to be lying, but why would he lie about that? He was a vampire. One who could've killed me ages ago but hadn't. He hadn't done anything to me except make me feel alive. "We didn't do that."

"*You* did nothing. But your kind did. Harlow, I brought you here for help. No, it probably wasn't the best idea, but you'd been poisoned with a potion, which means the witches or vampires or hybrids injected you with it when the Lair was attacked. I had to save you. I'll take the fall. I'll do whatever I need to do to repay them."

Staring into his green eyes, I saw the truth. Even in my weakened state, I was still strong enough to detect lies. He wasn't lying. He had never once told me a lie. I had never known a vampire who had been so kind or had dealt with so much pain. This man, this incredibly strong, sexy, passionate man stood before me baring his soul. He could easily kill me, but in everything he did, it was out of love. I finally understood what Dmitry, Trajan, and Mina had tried explaining to me.

I took a deep breath, and slowly made my way toward him. He was breathing hard, and all I wanted to do was touch his chest. I wanted to heal the scars and all the pain he had experienced. I wanted to finally show him what he meant to me.

Reaching up, I ran my hand over his long scars. Touching him sent shockwaves throughout me, awakening all of my senses. I had never felt anything like it in my existence. How was it possible that I needed him, a vampire, someone who was supposed to be my enemy? I wanted him, and as if he sensed my need, he leaned down and pressed his lips against mine. Cradling my face in his hands, he moved his mouth with mine with enough passion to set me on fire. My heart raced as his kiss knocked me into the door. His lips trailed down my neck, and I let out a breath. I reached down to his erect cock and stroked it. He moaned in my ear and he lifted me, carefully placing me on the bed. Climbing on top of me, he slipped his tongue inside my mouth and pressed his body to mine. The mattress was uncomfortable and noisy, but I didn't care. I just wanted to feel him inside me, yet unlike last time, he took it slow. I didn't understand the deliberateness of his movements, but it turned me on even more. He kissed his way from my neck to my stomach, including my scars. His hands roamed over my body, and once he removed my shirt, he squeezed and massaged my breasts.

He leaned down seizing a nipple in his hot mouth. His hand played with my other breast and wandered to my stomach. I had never felt anything like this. Sex was always quick and to the point, but Alaric was driving me wild with this slow way.

He dragged his hot tongue down to my stomach and he slowly opened my jeans, sliding them off of me. He kissed my inner thigh. He kissed just above my panties. On my hips. Skating that delicious tongue all over. It drove me crazy and I couldn't be still. He slowly slipped my panties down my legs inch by inch.

"You are so sexy," he growled as he kissed my inner thigh once more. He slid his tongue inside my wet pussy, and I gasped. He nibbled and sucked, and I wanted more. I tried directing him to my clit, but he removed my hands and continued pushing his tongue inside me. He kissed my thigh more and I couldn't catch my breath. His fingers rubbed through my slick folds, then he slipped a finger inside. He watched me as I moaned and trembled. He slipped another inside and as he slowly moved them in and out, he continued watching me squirm with a beautiful smirk across his face.

He scooted me closer to the edge of the bed and got down his knees. Finally, his mouth landed on my clit, sucking and biting and licking. He knew exactly how to make me feel good. I trembled involuntarily and moaned as heat filled me. His tongue flicked my clit, and I gripped his hair, pressing him harder against me.

"Alaric." I was flying high. He plunged two fingers inside my pussy and eased one in my ass as he sucked, using the right amount of pressure. I climbed higher, the rush fell over me like a warm euphoric blanket covering me.

"Fuck, you taste amazing." His fangs were extended, and the fierce look in his green eyes turned me on even more.

"Bite me," I breathed.

He stilled. "Are you sure?"

"Yes." His fingers still pumped in and out of me and I could feel myself climbing again. "Bite me, Alaric. Hard."

Watching him sink his sharp teeth into my inner thigh made me dizzy. With his fingers moving vigorously, it was like no other high I had ever felt. The fire of his venom slowly moved inside my veins. Colors exploded behind my eyelids like a kaleidoscope of my feelings for Alaric.

He covered me with his body, his hard cock poised at my entrance, and gazed into my eyes with such intensity. "No one has ever made me feel this way."

"What? Not even with Danielle?"

He shook his head. "No one, Harlow." Alaric slowly pushed his hard, long cock inside, filling me completely, and I moaned. I felt him throb. He moved slow, methodical, like he wanted to enjoy every second. His lips met mine in a hot kiss.

I squeezed his ass. "Fuck me, harder."

He slammed into me so hard, I thought the bed was about to break, I bit my lip to keep from screaming. He leaned down, his lips grazing my neck, and then I felt his sharp teeth against my skin. Chills rushed over me. As he pounded into me, I could feel his hot breath in my ear.

"I never wanted to hurt you, Harlow. Not you."

"I know."

"I love feeling you inside me."

"I love being inside you."

I lifted my legs around his waist as he deepened his thrusts. Groaning loudly, I didn't care who heard me. I couldn't be quiet, feeling this beautiful man inside me. Since I'd known him, he had always helped me and saved me. He had always made me feel incredible.

I put my hand to his chest and met his eyes.

He slowed to a stop. "What is it? Are you okay? I know you're still ill."

I shook my head. "Alaric, I need you."

CHAPTER NINETEEN
ALARIC

Hearing those words leave Harlow's mouth made him throb and succumb to an orgasm. Instead of pulling out of her, he rolled both of them onto his back, holding her on top. Her blonde hair tickled his chest. Their sweaty naked bodies pressed against each other, both panting, with him still inside her, still throbbing. His hands slipped over her ass, gripping it. He slid his finger inside her pussy, and dragged it up to her nether region, slowly slipping it inside.

She gasped and stared at him with those sexy ruby eyes.

"Your fucking eyes captivate me," he said as she began grinding against his cock. His finger moved in and out of her ass. He watched the blithe way she moved on top of him. The lustful way she looked at him. "You're fucking hot, Harlow. I can't get enough of you."

She cried out as she came once more over his hard cock. "No one's made me come as much as you have."

He growled, quickly positioning them so that she was on her hands and knees. In one swift movement, his cock thrust into her pussy. Again. And again. He reached around to her clit and slapped it once, twice, three times. He always wanted to make her feel good.

She gasped. "Harder."

He briefly hesitated, not wanting to make her sicker, but when she squirmed, he pounded into her so hard, watching her breasts bounce. He slapped her ass. He wasn't going to last long, and he sank his teeth into her shoulder as he spurted his seed inside her.

They fell to the bed, and he gathered her into his arms. She left feather light kisses on his face.

"How do you feel?"

"Very relaxed. And strong."

"Do you feel sick or anything?"

"No. Tired, but not like I did before. Did they say what was wrong?"

"Gemma said you were poisoned but had no other information."

"Gemma?"

"She took us in and created the antidote for you."

"Why did they seal the room?"

"Because they're afraid we'll kill them."

"That doesn't make sense. Can't witches kill us quickly?"

"One would think. I met Aria's friend, Lolly."

"Oh?"

"She wants me. She's only with the witches so she can be a part of this world somehow."

"That's fucked up. She clearly has issues."

"Yes, but maybe we can use it to our advantage."

"How?"

"You can enter her dreams and convince her to release us. We should get dressed though. Someone's walking toward the door."

They threw on clothes and someone knocked on the door before it opened.

Gemma and another witch with dark skin and gray hair walked inside. "Good morning. This is Ciara. She's the coven leader. We just came to check on you." Gemma's eyes fell on Harlow. "You look better."

"Thanks for healing me. What do you all want in return?"

"For you not to kill us?" She let out a nervous laugh.

Alaric wished he could compel the truth out of her, but witches were immune to compulsion. However, that was where Lolly came in handy. She wanted to be in the world, so be it.

"Why did you really lock us in here?" Harlow demanded.

"You should rest."

Harlow rushed up to Gemma, seizing her throat. "Tell me the truth."

Gemma scratched at Harlow's hands, her eyes switching from Ciara to Alaric for help. "Please. I can't breathe."

"I know, that's the point."

Ciara closed her eyes, and as a flash of blue light illuminated the room, a force so strong threw Harlow across the room, her back hitting the wall. Alaric moved toward Ciara, but she held up her hands. He knew witches could do damage to vampires. Instead of attacking, he checked on Harlow and helped her to her feet.

"Are you okay?"

"I'm fine."

"Look, we just want the truth," Alaric said. "We don't want to fight."

"We never wanted to be in the middle of this war," Ciara said. Her husky voice was eloquent, and she stood still, almost like a statue, but Alaric knew she could severely destroy both of them in a matter of seconds. "None of us did."

"Neither did we."

"Oh? Vampires started it."

"Who cares who started it," Harlow yelled. "Why are you keeping us here? What do you want from us?"

"We want the hybrids to die. You, Aria, and Caleb are our only hope to end them all. However, Grayson caught wind of Aria, and ever since he realized who she is, he wants to find her before us and kill her."

"What?" Harlow asked. "How the fuck is some human, and us, your only hope to end hybrids?"

"You are the missing piece to the spell. Her blood, a royal vampire's blood, and yours."

Alaric froze. Dammit. They had two out of the three standing in the room before them. "Well, you're a bit too late, because Aria is now a demon," Alaric said.

"Her blood will always remain pure. She may have traits of a demon, but she will never fully transition into one. Her blood prevents that."

"What's so special about everyone's blood?" he asked.

"Aria is a descendent of the Killian Coven."

"Killian Coven," Harlow repeated. "That name sounds familiar."

"It should. It's part of your history."

Alaric stilled as he saw the blood leave Harlow's face. "What does that mean?"

"Jacob Killian. The fucked-up scientist who created demons. He was a witch?"

"The one and only," Ciara said. "He created demons to kill off the vampires, but that didn't work. Our coven was the one who made Caleb into the vampire King."

"Why would you do that?"

"The King at the time forced witches to do his bidding. He had no heir, so he chose a pregnant woman to provide one. The King wanted someone to continue leading vampires to kill demons. With all of this terror that witches once created, we are here to end it."

"You create something and just like that want it to die?"

"We did not create them. Our ancestors did, and it was a mistake. It's unfortunate that some of our ancestors took liberties with their powers and used it for dark purposes. It's illegal in the witching world, but like anywhere else, criminals exist."

"We shouldn't be punished for your crimes," Harlow said, her voice amplifying. "That's why you locked us in here and healed me?"

Ciara shrugged. "We took advantage of the situation when you mentioned Aria's name. And when we saw you, we recognized you. You two fill a huge part of the spell. Once she arrives, we start the spell, and one by one, the hybrids die."

"Okay, why do you need Alaric and me? Why not Caleb?"

"Caleb is the true vampire King, but it appears that we have a royal vampire in our presence, and we believe he'll work just fine."

"A royal?"

"I was turned by someone with royal blood," Alaric admitted. "But why Harlow?"

Ciara turned to Harlow. "You were turned into a demon by an original demon."

"What are you talking about? I'm just a normal demon."

"Not so much. It's a shame no one told you about your past."

Harlow furrowed her eyebrows, trying to process everything.

"Okay so you try to kill Grayson's hybrids, but he will come after you and kill every single one of you like he did my coven and more."

"We want him to, but he won't kill us. We have a plan to kill him. Without his army of hybrids, he's nothing."

Alaric couldn't argue. "Okay. Why did you need to hold us hostage? We want Grayson and his hybrids dead, too."

"We can't have you running away from us."

"We all want the same thing, so we aren't going to run."

"You're willing to sacrifice yourself and your friends to end hybrids?"

"We have plenty of blood. We can sacrifice that."

"We need *all* your blood."

Harlow gasped. "You want us to just hand over our lives for you?"

"You said so yourself. You wanted Grayson and the hybrids dead. This is how you kill them."

"There has to be another way," Alaric said. He was not going to be held hostage by fucking witches until he just gave them his blood and life.

"That's why you poisoned me in battle. It was too dangerous to collect us then, so you poisoned me, knowing Aria had connections with witches. Knowing we'd eventually come to you for help, and in some sick twisted way, you use that as us giving in to your sacrifice."

"Yes, but we also had the twins lure her to us as well. So you see our plan worked."

"This is sick," Harlow said.

"So is making hybrid vampire demons. None of you should exist. It isn't natural. Nature did not create you. You are only science experiments made by sick and twisted people."

"You say that, but once you kill these hybrids and Grayson, you don't think some other sick psycho won't try the same thing?"

"We thought of that. We have plans to end the entire vampire and demon race. You've both used us to do your bidding one too many times. We will not bow down to you any longer."

"You want us to sacrifice ourselves to kill the hybrids, and you want to kill off the entire vampire and demon races?"

"It's a small price to pay, but this world doesn't need either of your kinds."

Harlow crossed her arms in front of her chest. "You call us the monsters, yet it was your kind who created us. You're the ones who created this chaos. You should die."

"And we intend to end it." Gemma smiled and left the room.

"She can't be serious," Harlow said. "We can't be sacrificed. There has to be another way to kill Grayson."

Alaric pulled Harlow into his arms. "We aren't going to die. We'll find another way."

CHAPTER TWENTY
HARLOW

Not only did they need to figure out a way to kill Grayson and the hybrids, they needed to protect themselves from the witches. Harlow took a deep breath. The witches had only saved her, so they could kill her. Yet demons were the monsters. Was it just the coven or was it all witches?

"Are you okay?" Alaric asked.

"I'm fine. Except for being held hostage. Oh, and having to sacrifice ourselves for this shit."

"We'll get out of this, I promise."

"Part of me wants to run away from all of this, Alaric. I don't want to sacrifice myself for my kind or yours. But the other part of me has to."

"I know the feeling."

"They can't possibly kill all vampires and demons. We have to warn Dmitry and Aria from stepping foot in this place."

"You have to convince Lolly to release us," he said. "She's the only option we have."

"I don't even know what she looks like."

Alaric placed his hands on both sides of my face and closed his eyes. An image appeared in my head of a woman with auburn hair that fell in long curly tendrils. Her brown eyes begged for excitement and she longed for an intense romance. She seemed a little pathetic, but I had known humans of her type before. They had no idea what they were getting into and usually ended up dead.

When he drew back, he looked at me expectantly. No one had ever been inside my mind before, certainly not like that. The connection was intense.

"Okay. I'll try my best."

"You'll do great. I can help you gain power, if you'd like." He grinned.

"You do alright." He did more than alright. He made me feel and see things I never thought were possible, especially for a demon.

In one swift movement, he had my back on the bed with him on top of me. Grinding against me, he nibbled on my ear. "Lolly wants to hook up with me, so maybe work that in your angle."

Alaric kissed my neck.

"Not everyone wants you."

He raised an eyebrow. "Everyone wants this." He slid his hand up my shirt and pinched my nipple until it hardened.

"You're quite full of yourself."

His hands wandered down inside my pants. "Why shouldn't I be?"

"It's not as attractive as you might think."

Sinking two fingers inside my heat, he chuckled. "Feels pretty attractive to me."

I shrugged. "I'm just desperate is all. I am a succubus after all. Don't you know we'll fuck anything?"

He jerked my pants off and spread my legs. His green eyes swept over my naked body. Studying my wetness, his fangs grew and the demon inside me ached for him. "Well from now on, this is my pussy." He pumped his fingers inside me, hitting me in the right spot. "If you need to fuck, I'm the only one."

"You can't tell me what to do." I pushed him off me and straddled him. "Besides, your dick is mine." Reaching inside his pants, I grabbed his hard cock in my hand. I pulled down his pants, freeing his hard cock. Alaric was incredibly hot. Everything about him made me hot. I wanted to suck him and make him feel as good as me, and demons never went down on their victims or vice versa. One would think we'd make sex last as long as possible, but we usually had so much of it, and we had to get our killings done.

I lowered myself so that his cock poised at my mouth.

"Harlow," he hesitated.

I liked his long length and he sucked in a breath. Teasing him with my tongue, I watched him squirm. Grabbing him at the base, I took him as far as I could and sucked him hard and light. He fisted my hair.

"Fuck that feels good."

I didn't stop. He bucked and pulled my hair. I straddled him, easing onto his hard, long cock, filling me at the hilt. The demon raged and wanted it hard and fast, like always. Alaric gripped my hips and flipped us over. Plunging into me hard, he lifted my hips and my legs rested around his waist. His thrusts weren't gentle, and I loved it. I lost myself in the pure ecstasy of being with a man who knew exactly how to make me feel good. My breathing labored, and I didn't hold back this time. A scream tore from my throat as I came. An intoxicating rapture pulsated inside me and I wanted more.

"I want to feed from you," I whispered.

He slowed to a steady pace and watched me with those mesmerizing green eyes. "You want my blood?"

"Yes. I want every bit of you."

"Fuck, you surprise me all the time. Are you sure it's okay?"

"Alaric," I begged.

He bit his wrist and placed it across my mouth. As he pumped into me, I drank, letting his blood satiate my need. Warmth and power burst throughout me. Alaric leaned down and sank his teeth into my neck. Fire ignited inside me. Pinwheels of colors erupted behind my eyelids and I was climbing. The demon was close to being satisfied.

As if he read my mind, Alaric picked up his pace fucking me so hard, I felt the bed creak as if it would break. When he came, I felt him throb inside of me, but he didn't leave. He stayed like that.

After all this time, I never wanted him to complete me, but he did, and I was hopelessly falling in love with a vampire.

CHAPTER TWENTY-ONE
ALARIC

Being inside Harlow completed him. Alaric never thought a woman would make him feel like that, but she did. He was still hard as a rock, and it was obvious they wanted more, but they had to figure out what their next move would be. He reluctantly pulled out of her.

Harlow's red eyes peered at Alaric, and a sly smile stretched across her face. "Your dick is mine," she said.

I raised an eyebrow. "What?"

"You heard me," she said as she stood up, walking toward the bathroom like some sexy feline. "I own your cock."

The sultry way she said *cock* made him twitch. He followed her, watching her turn on the shower. "We already had this discussion and I've told you that's my pussy."

She rolled her eyes.

Alaric grabbed her, pressing her against the shower door, and slapped her across each ass cheek. He dipped down, spread her pussy lips, and fucked her with his tongue. Her body trembled, and it made his dick even harder. He couldn't wait to be inside her and feel every inch of that hot, wet pussy around him again.

He growled as he stood, bending her just right. The water fell between them and he pushed his cock deep inside her. She felt so fucking good. He grabbed her hair and pulled as he slammed into her. He swore she got wetter and wetter with each stroke.

"Alaric," she moaned.

He slapped her ass hard and slipped his thumb inside that tight hole. "Scream, Harlow. Let everyone know how good I make you feel."

She whimpered, and he pumped harder. When she finally came, her body slacked against him. Tingles encased his body as he came inside her. She wasn't a rebound at all, and he wasn't just a fuck for her. He was falling in love with her.

CHAPTER TWENTY-TWO
HARLOW

Searching for a woman's mind who I had never met before proved to be quite difficult. Alaric had given me a full image of her but being in a house of witches and their cloaking spells and protection spells didn't help. After the fourth time of trying, I stopped.

"I can't find her."

"Let me see if I can hear her." Alaric closed his eyes, and I knew he was searching for her sounds. If she was breathing heavily, yet steadily, it meant she was asleep. "I found her. She's asleep."

Closing my eyes, I focused on the woman. Finally, I found her and opened the door to her mind. Inside the dream, I walked toward her. She was by herself at a desk worrying about something. No witch was there with her, and I wondered why she didn't dream about her boyfriend.

When she saw me, she jumped back, and gasped. "I wasn't expecting you." Her face fell, a clear indication that she was thinking about Alaric and wanted to have a sex dream about him. "Where is Alaric?"

"He isn't an incubus. Only demons can enter dreams. Look, I don't have much time, but you want to save Alaric, no?"

Lolly stood and pleaded with her eyes. "I do, but, how can I? When I saw him, I had never felt anything like it. I-I think I love him."

"Then you must help him. He's in trouble. You have to release us."

"They'll kill me."

Rolling my eyes internally, I used Alaric's tactic. If it would save us, I would do it. "Alaric will keep you safe. He told me himself he felt something when you came to him. He can't explain it, but he needs you, Lolly. If you release us, he will protect you forever. He would never let anything happen to you."

She smiled like a woman in love. "I have to get away from these witches. They constantly fuck with my mind and control me. Zeke doesn't love me. He controls me. They're just using me to get to Aria."

"It's okay. We'll get you out of here, but you have to help us. You have to find a way to lift the spell for our room."

"How do I do that?"

"I don't know. Create a sleeping potion for Gemma. She's the one who cast the spell. Also, we need to warn Aria and Dmitry."

"Why would I want to do that? She tried to kill me."

"Aria is your best friend. She didn't know what she was doing. She's just as lost as you are. Besides, she's in danger, too. Your witches want us all dead."

She shook her head. "No! They can't kill Alaric. Not him."

I wasn't sure the plan would work as she was so set on Alaric and his safety and no one else, but I trusted Alaric to keep the rest of us safe. "Then you'll help us?"

"Yes, of course. I know where they keep the potions. I'll slip it into her food for dinner. When she falls asleep, I'll come to you and we'll escape."

"Can you leave during the day and warn Aria? She's on her way here."

"She'll kill me."

"No, she won't. Dmitry is with her, but she's controlled now."

Lolly nodded. "Okay. I'll set out once I wake."

"If you get caught, just make up something."

"Of course. Alaric really feels that way about me?" she asked, hopeful.

"Yes. You're the one for him. I feel it."

"What about you?"

"Are you kidding me? He's a vampire."

Her wide smile returned, and I left her dream.

"Well?" Alaric asked.

"What the fuck did you do to her? She is completely obsessed with you."

"I told you. So, she'll help us?"

"More like, she'll help you, and hopefully everything else will fall into place."

"Good."

"By the way, she thinks you feel the same way toward her, so have fun with that when we get out of here."

"I'll compel her. Once we're out of here and we get far enough away from this place."

"This better work, Alaric."

He cupped my chin, forcing me to meet his eyes. "Do you trust me?"

"Yes, I do."

"That's all it takes. We'll survive this, Harlow. I promise. We're strong enough."

Falling in love with a vampire was the last thing I had ever expected to do, but that was exactly what was happening. This vampire had risked so much for me, and we weren't supposed to feel anything for each other, but we did. Who knew if we would ever survive this, and if we did would we still feel this strongly for each other?

CHAPTER TWENTY-THREE
ALARIC

Alaric's throat burned. He needed to feed soon. It had been a few days since the witches held them hostage. He didn't care about himself, not until Harlow was better. He hoped Lolly would help them even if he had to pretend. He pulled Harlow's sleeping body closer to him, loving her warmth against his skin. He loved listening to her breathe. He never expected to fall in love again, but he had. With a demon. Someone who surprised him and stirred long lost emotions within him. Her strength and strong-willed nature amazed him and turned him on. She was independent and fierce. She challenged him and gave him a reason to fight. After losing his family, he hadn't wanted to fight. He went along with it hoping that feeling would return. He hated the despair and did his best not to focus on it. He had been so close to leaving the group, but now he couldn't even fathom that thought. Alaric was in love.

They had to find and kill Grayson. If they killed Grayson, it would end the war. The hybrids wouldn't have a leader. They would just be crazed maniacs running through cities, which they were already doing. Once they figured out a way to kill the hybrids, they would have to contain the witches.

Alaric hoped like hell they hadn't put any other spells on him or Harlow. He knew how sneaky they could be. They could track or bind them. It never ceased to amaze him all the things witches could do. Shit, they created demons. For that, he was thankful, only because it brought Harlow to him.

Harlow stirred in his arms and opened her eyes, the light from the moon glinting on them. "Why are you awake?"

"I don't trust these witches, so I'm not sleeping."

"Have you been up the whole time we've been here?"

"Yes ma'am."

"You're ridiculous."

"Maybe. But you love it."

She smiled. "Well, the accommodations for being a witch prisoner are certainly nicer than when I was for the vampires."

Alaric tensed. He hated thinking his own kind had anything to do with torturing or hurting her. Had they hurt her like the demons did with him? "What did they do to you?"

Harlow took a minute to respond. He wasn't sure he should've asked, but it was too late. "They would shoot me to see what slowed me down. They took my blood by slicing open my arms. They held me in a dark cell with my hands in shackles, stabbing me, hitting me, just to see how long it took me to heal."

He let out a long sigh.

Fuck.

"Did they ever force themselves—"

"No," she quickly said. "They knew that would give me strength. They would bring a human but wouldn't let me ingest all of their life energy."

He pulled her closer to him. "I'm sorry."

"Don't be. Demons probably weren't any better on you."

"No, they weren't."

"How come your scars never healed?"

"They wouldn't let them. They had devices made by witches that prevented healing."

Harlow kissed him softly. "No more torture," she whispered. "Get some sleep. I'll keep watch."

"You'd do that for me?"

He knew she would do anything for him by the deep look in her eyes. Harlow moved on top of him, straddling him. Her lips met his sealing them in a hot kiss. As she slid her wet heat over his hard cock, he moaned.

"Fuck, you always feel so good."

She moved in a steady rhythm up and down as he gripped her ass.

He bit his wrist and offered it to her. She took it as he sank his teeth into her neck. Fire ignited inside him as she writhed harder. She cried out and he soon followed.

Harlow lay next to him and brought his head against her chest. "Get some rest. I'll stare at your naked body."

He chuckled. "It's just sex for you I see."

"I told you. Besides, demons are selfish monsters, remember?"

"Not gonna let that go?"

"I might."

Running her fingers through his hair made him close his eyes.

CHAPTER TWENTY-FOUR
HARLOW

The night finally arrived, and I was on edge. Alaric was, too, but he was also hungry. I couldn't believe he hadn't slept the whole time, except today.

We waited for Lolly to come to us. We needed to find Aria and Dmitry and the fact that they hadn't shown up scared me. Where were they? Had Grayson caught them?

"What is it?" Alaric asked.

"Where are Aria and Dmitry? Wouldn't they have been here by now?"

"They're fine. We'll find them."

I stood from the bed. "Where is Lolly? They found out. They're going to keep us here until their sick ritual happens."

Alaric stopped me from pacing. "We're going to be fine."

"How can you be so sure?"

"I have to be."

We waited anxiously for Lolly to come to us, but the more we waited, the more impatient I became.

It was well after midnight that someone softly knocked on the door. Alaric opened it, and Lolly ran straight into his arms. The demon in me wanted to seize her neck and tear her head off. I turned around knowing my eyes were red. She was helping us, and I had to play along. I had to play nice, but I didn't want to. Seeing another woman in love with Alaric touch him, drove me to a dark place. What was that feeling? Demons felt nothing. So, we'd been told our entire existence. But I felt everything with him. Were we told that because we couldn't control emotions, so we turned them off?

"I drugged Gemma, and the spell is broken for the room," Lolly said. Her eyes were wide, and she panted. "We have to go now. And quietly."

Alaric flashed me those green eyes and I saw the intense look, knowing I was his and only his. But I hated seeing him take Lolly's hand as she led us through the hallway and downstairs. Right through the empty bar. Where was everyone? The Downward Spiral partied on for hours. Maybe witches didn't party like we did. We ran out the door into the cold night. Snow crunched under our feet as we ran. Alaric had to lift the weak human because she was too slow for us, and it angered the demon in me. If I focused on running, maybe I wouldn't want to kill her. She had saved us after all.

I didn't know how far we ran, but we slowed down once we saw a small cottage of sorts hidden away in the woods. It boggled my mind why we came upon random cottages in the woods. Had humans always lived like that? I was used to thriving cities.

How had Alaric known where to go? Or had Lolly told him? He set Lolly down on her feet and she looked up at him with annoying googly eyes. We walked inside the cottage and Aria and Dmitry stood. I let out a sigh of relief.

"Lolly?" Aria said, clearly confused to see her. Hadn't Lolly warned them earlier today?

"Hi Aria."

"Good to see you two are safe," Dmitry said. "How did you know we were here?"

"She showed me," Alaric said. "Why are you here? Why didn't you come find us at the witch's bar?"

"How did you know where we were, Lolly?"

Seizing her arm, I turned her to face me. She gasped, and her brown eyes widened. "What the fuck is going on?"

"I-I went out today and saw Dmitry and Aria, but I couldn't say anything because the witches have a tight leash on me, so I tried to give a sign for you to wait here until we came."

"We got the note," Dmitry said.

"That was you?" Aria asked, shocked. "Why are you helping us?"

"I don't want to be with the witches any longer. They spellbind me and make me do things."

The way Aria studied her made me wary, but I waited.

"What happened with the witches?" Dmitry asked.

"They need our blood and Aria's to finish some fucking ritual. Basically, in order to kill the hybrids, they need blood from a demon, a vampire, and Aria, who is a descendent of the Killian Coven."

Aria gasped. "What? How did I not know about this?"

"I don't think many people did. Apparently, I'm made from an original demon and Alaric has royal vampire blood."

"What do we do?"

"You should give yourselves up," Lolly said.

"What?" Aria held open her mouth.

"There's no way to beat the witches. They have vast power. I've seen them bring vampires to their knees. They manipulate me."

"We're building an army, so we can defeat them," Dmitry said.

"You don't get it. Witches created demons. Don't you think they can kill you off? Hybrids are out there killing thousands of innocent people. Don't you care about that?

Or are you all so self-involved, you don't care about the world?" Lolly shouted.

"Why should we give a fuck about the world?" Harlow asked. "It's done nothing to us but try to kill us. Whose side are you on?"

"I'm on your side," she said glancing at Alaric. She had already given us what we needed, so why was she still around and why hadn't he compelled her yet?

"What took you two so long?" Alaric asked.

"Witches cloaked the bar," Aria said. "We found this cabin and have been kinda staying here."

Anger welled inside me. "You two have been having a fucking lover's vacation while we've been held hostage?"

"How the fuck could we have found you, Harlow?" Dmitry snapped. "Everything around here is invisible. We didn't know where you were."

I understood, but I didn't want to. "Well, we'd better get far away from here because they want us."

Glass shattered, and as I turned, flames shot up from the broken window. I glanced outside and saw several people cluttered in the front of the cottage. Through the fire, I recognized a familiar face. Trajan. And next to him stood Grayson.

CHAPTER TWENTY-FIVE
ALARIC

"Oh god, the witches found us!" Lolly screamed. Alaric had to compel her, but as fire and smoke surrounded the five of them with no way out, compulsion had to wait. "We have to go! Come on." She motioned for them to follow her into the lone bedroom. Smoke billowed inside making it difficult to see.

Alaric had to stop all of it. He had to keep Harlow safe from the witches.

Lolly got down on her knees and pushed a rug out of the way, revealing a trap door. She lifted it. "Everyone inside. I promise it'll lead us out of here."

They exchanged looks with each other, wary of trusting her.

"Scream," Alaric said. "I need everyone to scream so it sounds like we're burning alive."

The fire had inched its way inside the bedroom, and they needed to hurry to escape the blinding heat.

"Do it!"

The four of them screamed and Lolly slowly climbed down into the hole. Aria's scream faded as she followed, then Dmitry.

Harlow's brown eyes met his, and he hated the sinking feeling in his stomach. "Should we?"

Alaric knew she would hate him, but she had to stay alive. He seized her, pressing her into him, and kissed her hard. "I love you, Harlow. Forever."

"I love you." She furrowed her eyebrows, but he helped her into the trap door.

"Keep her safe," he said and closed the door, quickly pushing the bed over it. The smoke overwhelmed him, and he stumbled. Flames latched onto his arm searing his flesh. He had to push himself to get out. With every bit of strength he had, he leapt out the window and landed hard on the snow, coughing. The snow doused the fire and he felt relief.

Snow crunched as someone approached him. "Are you the lone survivor?" He recognized the voice. Grayson. What the fuck was he doing there?

"They're all dead," Alaric said, rolling onto his back.

Grayson smiled. His long, brown hair fell past his shoulders and his beard was tousled. He reeked of the same pungent herb as witches.

"Including the human."

"Human?" his voice rang with surprise.

Alaric secretly loved the way Grayson's veins bulged from hearing the news, but he knew he shouldn't have admitted it.

Fuck.

"This displeases me. Too bad. I could've turned her." He kneeled next to Alaric, and Alaric held himself up on his elbows. When he looked up, he saw Trajan. What the fuck was going on?

"It's good to see you again, Alaric. Shame what happened to your coven and all. I had hoped we could all come to an agreement on things. But it looks as though that won't happen."

Shit. Alaric knew what he had to do. "I'll do whatever you want."

"Oh? Seems as if you were protecting the one thing I needed, but she's dead now."

"We had to get away from the witches. I had intended to kill her since the witches intend to kill us all."

"Oh, they do? And how do they intend to do that?"

"I don't know. They need blood from Aria, a demon, and a vampire to complete the sacrifice to kill the hybrids. I don't know how they plan to kill off the rest of us."

"Hmm. You may actually have a purpose. Where do these witches stay?"

"They've cloaked it."

"But it's around here."

"Yes."

Alaric needed Grayson to believe him. Somehow, he needed to kill Grayson, but he had a group of lackeys it seemed. And Trajan was one of them.

CHAPTER TWENTY-SIX
HARLOW

As soon as the trap door closed, I lurched toward it, but arms held me back. I clawed at them, trying everything I could to open it. Alaric had closed the door leaving us inside while he left.

"Harlow, stop!" Dmitry held her. "We need to go."

"No. We can't leave him," I shouted. "They're going to kill him."

"We'll get him back."

"Fuck you." I pushed at him, but he was much stronger than me. "You would go back if it was Aria."

He sighed, knowing I was right. "We've got to keep all of you safe."

"That was the most romantic thing anyone's ever done for me." Lolly wept.

I turned and slapped her across the face. Aria pulled me away from her. The demon inside raged, and I knew my eyes were red. I easily fought off Aria, but Dmitry restrained me again.

"What the fuck is your problem?" Lolly demanded, rubbing her cheek.

Aria grabbed her hand and pulled her through the dark tunnel away from us. I had no idea where it led, and I wondered how Lolly knew about it if she was kept under lock and key.

Breathing hard, I clenched my fists and punched the wall.

Fuck Alaric. He promised everything would be okay and that he needed me forever. He swore he loved me, but he left me to join Grayson. No one else saw who was out there. They all thought it was the witches. He had to have known Grayson would attack. Why else would he have deserted us?

None of it was real. I couldn't believe I fell in love with a vampire and his lies. But what could he have gained? Or what was he trying to accomplish with me? He had brought me to the witches to save me.

Dmitry clutched my hand as we lingered back from Aria and Lolly. He never told me to calm down or tried to give me some fake ass pep talk. I had fallen in love with a vampire who had risked his life for us. I refused to believe he was on Grayson's side now.

Demons didn't cry, and if we did, it was in the most private way. Anger was a good way to ease any sadness, but we had been taught for so long that we weren't humans and we didn't have the same feelings. But we were made from humans, the emotional creature. Emotions ran rampant within us. We just never knew how to control them like vampires. At least, I didn't know how. And if Dmitry wasn't helping me, I would've killed Lolly and Aria.

I needed Alaric. I needed to know he was okay. I couldn't think of him burning alive, but the image flashed in my mind like a beacon of horror. An ache punched me in the chest and pulsated throughout me. I hated the pain. The worst was not knowing what had happened to him.

"We have to go back, D."

"We can't."

"I have to know. None of this feels right."

"What are you talking about?"

"I saw Trajan and Grayson."

"What?"

"Those weren't witches. They were hybrids. How did they find us? How did Lolly know there was a trap door that was attached to a tunnel? What if she's leading us right back to the witches?"

"Why are you always paranoid?"

"Probably because everyone wants us dead."

"How could you see Trajan or Grayson through all that smoke and fire? Are you sure you saw them?"

"I fucking saw him, Dmitry." I placed my hands on his head giving him the image.

Shock appeared in his dark eyes. "Fuck. What is he doing? Where are the others?"

"We have to go back. We have to follow them."

"Where does this tunnel go?" Dmitry shouted through the tunnel at Lolly.

Aria and Lolly turned back and moved closer to us.

"I've never seen the end of it, but the witches always told me to use it if I ever got into any trouble."

I froze. "This place is probably spelled."

"Fuck," Dmitry spat.

"What does that matter?" Lolly asked.

"Witches can lock us into places," Aria said.

"Same way they locked us in that room. We're going up there."

"Shit, Harlow."

"If the Dominus still exists, I'm still a leader, especially now that Trajan betrayed us. We're going back up there and if we get into trouble, I will get us out. I have to know if Alaric *betrayed* us, too." I stumbled over the words.

"I doubt Alaric betrayed us, Harlow," Aria said. "If he thought the witches were out there, maybe he was sacrificing himself to save us."

"I still have to know. And we don't know how safe this tunnel really is for us."

Dmitry met my eyes, and after a moment he nodded. "Lead the way."

"We're following *her*?" Lolly scoffed. "She's going to get us killed."

I turned to face her. "I'll be the first to go and inspect so your precious life will be spared."

"I would just tell them you held me hostage."

"Lolly?" Aria said, dismayed.

"Alaric was talking about me when he said to keep her safe. You told me yourself that he loves me and that he would do anything for me. And he died keeping me safe."

Dmitry grabbed me and pulled me away. "Don't tell her the truth yet. She may still turn on us."

He slowly pushed open the trap door and looked around. "It's daylight."

Daylight meant only half of our enemies would be out, but witches liked to hide a lot. Dmitry opened the door all the way and out poured black billowing gray ash in a cloud. Holding out his hand for me, I took it and he helped lift me into the burned and charred bedroom. The stone walls were the only thing standing. My eyes scanned the room urgently searching for any clues.

I saw the broken window, rushed toward it, and when I looked out, I saw the perfect layer of snow was disturbed as if someone jumped out the window and landed in it. Following the trail, it led through the woods.

"There's a trail. They went through the woods," I told them as they all finished climbing out of the hole.

"Lolly, you have to find a safe place," Aria said. "You can't come with us. It's too dangerous."

"Didn't you hear Alaric? He said to keep me safe."

Gripping the windowsill, it broke under my strength. "He's dead," I snapped as I turned back to her. "So, there's no reason to keep you alive."

Aria moved in front of Lolly. "We have to keep her safe."

"And we will," Dmitry said. "But she can't come with us."

"I just helped them escape the witches. I think I'm fairly capable of handling myself."

"Around hungry vampires and rabid hybrids? You wouldn't last a second."

"Where am I supposed to go?" Tears clouded her eyes, trying to make us pity her, but we were demons. We were good at ignoring crying humans. Except Dmitry, who had fallen in love with one. "I can't go back to the witches. They will kill me."

"She could go back to our hideout," Aria said. "I can take her."

"We shouldn't be separated."

"Dmitry, I will be fine. Besides, I can't go to Grayson. He may think I'm dead."

"Maybe he thinks we're all dead," I told them, staring out the window again. "If we show up, he'll never suspect it. We have to follow this trail before it snows again."

"I will take her," Dmitry said.

I sighed. "And then what? You can't be out in this yourself."

"We'll stay there and wait for a signal. If Mina and Caleb gathered an army, maybe they're hiding out there, too."

"They were with Dani and Trajan. Now Trajan is with Grayson. What if they're all dead?"

"Don't think like that, Harlow."

I turned back to Dmitry. "Time is wasting now. Let's just stick together. We'll work better in numbers. If all else fails, you can turn Lolly into a demon." I pushed past them through the charred remains of the cottage, tired of the waiting and smelling the burned stench. I needed to find Alaric and save him, even if it killed me.

CHAPTER TWENTY-SEVEN
ALARIC

Just before the sun began to rise, Grayson had moved all of the hybrids, and Alaric, to some underground lair. It kind of reminded Alaric of the Underground. He missed his old place with windows that protected them from the sun. He loved peering out at the city and really wanted to take Harlow there, but it no longer existed. Had Grayson rebuilt his own version, or had he taken over another vampire's coven?

Alaric needed to feed. The burning in his throat had magnified, and he was sure Grayson hadn't stored any blood for his hybrids. Why would he when they could attack entire cities for food?

He sat among a group of hybrids, wondering what Grayson would use him for. Alaric looked up and saw Caroline, Danielle's friend and Sawyer's lover. She was a hybrid, and even though he knew she was stronger, the sadness she held in her eyes said otherwise. He got to his feet and made his way toward her.

"Caroline?"

She met his eyes with surprise and crossed her arms in front of her chest. "Alaric."

"What happened?"

"Nothing."

"How did you become a hybrid?"

"You know exactly how. I thought you had died that night at the Underground."

"Sawyer's okay. He's been looking for you."

She cleared her throat. "He needs to move on. Besides, Trajan already filled me in, but he's nothing to me."

Alaric knew damn well that she hadn't meant that, but under Grayson, he knew she had to make up lies.

He saw Trajan walk by and he clenched his teeth. Trajan paused in front of him.

"What the fuck do you want?" Alaric asked.

"Who was in that cottage with you?"

"Who the fuck do you think? They're dead now, in case you give a shit."

Trajan squared his shoulders and snatched Alaric up to his feet, dragging him down a hallway. Alaric couldn't fight back too much since Trajan was a hybrid and he was a starving vampire.

He punched Trajan in the jaw, but it only made Trajan shove him against a wall, baring his fangs. His eyes turned red, but it was different than Harlow's eyes.

"There's nothing we can do, Alaric. This is it. Join Grayson or die."

"Is that what you told Danielle? Or did you fake all that shit with her?"

Trajan threw his fist into Alaric's face and slammed his head into wall. Alaric was weak and needed blood. Fighting back wasn't an option. "You have to join, Alaric," Trajan whispered. "It's the only way to beat this."

"You want me to become a hybrid?"

"You may not need to."

"Why are you here? Why did you join?"

"Because I'm fucking sired asshole."

Alaric pushed him away. "What?"

"We all are."

"What the fuck does that even mean?"

"Means we do whatever he wants, whether we want to or not. I have no choice in the matter. I didn't desert Danielle by my own accord. I had to."

"How the fuck does he control you?"

"His blood made me. It's like being constantly compelled."

"Shit. We need to end this."

"If you think you're going to be able to kill Grayson, you got another thing coming."

"If we don't, the witches will."

Trajan scoffed. "I highly doubt they'll even come close. Besides, you can't kill him."

"Says who?"

"Says me. I won't allow you to kill him."

Alaric froze. "Did you kill Danielle and the rest?"

"I would never kill her. I can't help what I do. We have been sworn to protect Grayson and we will do whatever it takes."

"So if Danielle tried to kill Grayson what would you do? Would you kill her?"

"We are forced to do whatever it takes. You don't get it, do you? None of this matters. You can't kill Grayson because all of the hybrids would die."

"I think I could live with that."

"You don't give a shit about anything do you? Harlow's dead and you don't care."

Alaric swung his fist into Trajan's face. Trajan grappled him to the ground until they were pulled apart and Grayson walked up.

"Leave him alone," Grayson said, and Trajan obeyed. "I think you will make an excellent hybrid, Alaric."

"I'll never become one of your minions."

Grayson sneered. "We'll see. It's almost time for us to

seek out the witches."

Alaric looked around and saw the hybrids, hungry for blood. Blood. Alaric needed to feed. His mouth watered at the thought. He was withering and hated the weakness. He hated how much he missed Harlow and knew she was pissed at him for leaving like that, but he had no choice. He had to keep her safe, and if she were smart, she would keep moving away from the witches and hybrids. Hybrids that were sired to Grayson, which meant they did every single thing he told them to do. They were stronger than any vampire or demon. How the fuck would he survive the war? How would he avoid being turned into a hybrid?

None of them were safe.

CHAPTER TWENTY-EIGHT
HARLOW

The bright sun reflected on the snow, giving me a headache. I ventured out of the cabin, keenly aware of any possible sounds from witches in the woods. If all else failed, I would use Lolly as bait. The snow cooled my skin, but the heat from the sun warmed me. Not like Alaric. I missed him and hated that I had gotten attached to someone. Could demons really feel that way. It was all new to me.

"We'll find him," Dmitry said as he matched my stride. Aria and Lolly were a little way in front of us. Better for Lolly to be far away from me.

I sighed. "I'm not thinking about him. Is that what you and everyone else do? Only think of your lover and nothing else?"

Dmitry chuckled. "No, but it's okay to let yourself feel, Harlow."

"I can't allow myself that."

"Why?"

"Because, Dmitry. If I did that now and something happened to him, I don't know what I would do."

"He's going to be fine."

"You don't know that."

"No, I don't."

"What if the rest of our group is dead? Why is Trajan with Grayson? He keeps betraying us."

"I don't know what he's up to. I'm not going to think the others are dead."

Dmitry and Mina had been friends for so long, I didn't want to see what it would do to him if he lost her. I wasn't sure what we were going to do once we found the hybrids' hideout. There were only three of us and a human. We needed to find the rest, or at least find more demons and vampires.

"Shouldn't we go back to the cabin to see if the rest of them are with an army at least?"

"If we waste time, the hybrids will move."

"They'll attack the witches. Why do we need them alive?"

"Despite their reasons, they did save you."

"Alaric saved me," I corrected him.

"We can't have them attacking the witches, and we have to keep you, Alaric, and Aria away from them."

"Okay, say we defeat the hybrids and Grayson. We'll still need to fight the witches."

"One thing at a time."

The more I thought about it though, the more I needed to figure out a plan. Maybe I could stay behind and watch the hybrids while Dmitry, Aria, and Lolly went back to the cabin for the others. We needed an army. As we moved forward, a plan formed inside my head.

"Dmitry, you three need to collect the army. I'll stay behind and watch the hybrids."

"You're joking. There is no way I'm leaving you here alone."

"It'll be fine."

"And the second you see Alaric, you will blow your cover and they'll kill you."

"I won't. We can't face them alone. You think we can take them?"

"No, I don't."

"This is the only way. As the leader of the demons, this is what we're doing. You are a leader, too. You need to lead them back here for us to attack the hybrids. If we kill Grayson, they all die."

"But what about Trajan?" Dmitry asked.

"What about him? He made his decision."

"What if they turn Alaric into a hybrid?"

I knew that was an option. "I'll find out. I don't know how, but I will."

"I don't like this plan at all."

"You don't have to, but this is for the best."

He studied me. "You haven't been feeling tired at all? I mean, the witches completely healed you?"

"Yes, they did. I'll be fine. I promise. Besides, it's daylight so the hybrids will be hiding for a while. You all can be back here in time for them to start moving again."

Dmitry let out a long sigh. "Don't attack them or rush up to Alaric. Just follow them at a distance. They can probably hear better than we can."

"I know. I'll be safe."

"Why don't you stay in the burned cabin? They may pass through here again."

"I'll clean up the tracks. Just hurry back, okay?"

"You got it." He drew me into an embrace and kissed my forehead. I waited until Dmitry, Aria, and Lolly were ahead to clear the tracks, but the sky turned gray and I knew another storm was about to blow through.

CHAPTER TWENTY-NINE
ALARIC

Hybrids impatiently waited until the sun set. Alaric didn't know what they would do, even if they found the witches. Grayson hadn't forced him to become a hybrid. Yet.

"What's the plan?" Alaric asked Trajan.

"We're going to kill the witches."

Alaric didn't know if the hybrids could defeat the witches, and he didn't understand why Grayson wanted to kill them. Hadn't they been working together? Weren't they all on the same side?

"Why does Grayson want them dead?"

"He doesn't need them anymore. And he knows they're trying to kill all of us and him."

"How did he find that out?"

"He has eyes and ears everywhere, Alaric. Try paying attention more. I don't know what's going to happen with you, though," Trajan added.

"What do you mean?"

"You're not coming with us. Looks like we're going to keep you locked up. Depending on how this goes, you may be locked up forever."

"What the fuck is that supposed to mean?"

Trajan held a smug grin and moved closer to Alaric. "Grayson told me to lock you up and that you're my responsibility."

"Still afraid Danielle will come back to me?" Seeing Trajan's jaw clench brought him satisfaction. He found it ridiculous that he still could get to Trajan with that threat. Like Alaric would ever take Danielle back. He only wanted Harlow. He needed her, but he would be damned if he let Trajan know that.

"Dani would never go back to a fucked-up loser like you. You're not strong enough for her."

"Think she'll even consider you after you betrayed her. Again?"

Trajan slammed his fist into Alaric's jaw. The fighting with him had gotten old. How the fuck was Trajan ever a leader with that temper? Alaric didn't fight back. It was pointless, and if he was going to be locked up forever, why would he fight back? He rubbed his jaw as Trajan jerked him up and pulled him down a hallway. Throwing him into a concrete cell, Trajan locked the door, and lifted a gun.

"Hope you enjoy your stay." He fired the gun twice, hitting Alaric in the chest and stomach. He was familiar with the bullets as they were something the demons created for vampires. It made their blood solidify if they stayed in the bloodstream too long.

Trajan walked away as Alaric fell to his knees. He had to remove the bullets. Digging into his chest, ignoring the intense pain, he felt the bullet and grabbed it. He tossed it on the ground, but as he reached for the other one, his eyes fell heavy and he collapsed, feeling his blood coagulating.

CHAPTER THIRTY
HARLOW

I waited in the cabin until the sun disappeared behind the horizon. As I stepped outside, a gust of icy wind greeted me. The snow swirled in a fury under the darkened sky. I needed to find a place to hide and watch the army pass through. It felt like I waited for hours, and I started to freeze. The cold never bothered me, but after the witches fucked with me, I seemed to have all sorts of issues. What had they done to me?

I heard crunching in the snow off in the distance and I froze. Lowering myself further into the forest, I watched a group trudge through the snow. I was anxious to pounce on them, but I had to wait. I had to find Alaric. The snow was thick in the air, but I forced myself to make out faces. Grayson. Trajan. Then I saw him, and my heart stopped. Alaric was completely limp. Trajan was dragging him through the snow as if he was dead. He didn't move. My blood turned cold and feelings overwhelmed me. I had never felt whatever this dead feeling was. Maybe he was just unconscious. Alaric couldn't be dead. But Grayson needed the three of us dead. Had they killed Alaric and were going to prance him around on the witch's doorstep?

Nausea roiled around in my stomach. Not like before when I had no energy. This was different. This was new. My stomach felt as if I had swallowed a thousand pounds of flesh. Pain stabbed my chest, and something pricked at the corners of my eyes. When I touched my face, it was wet. Goddammit. I was crying over a fucking vampire. A vampire who saved me. A vampire who loved me. Who never treated me like a monster. Alaric had risked his life for all of us, not just me. He saved me and made me feel things I had never felt.

"Interesting. I never thought a demon could cry." The voice startled me, and as I turned around, I let out a defeated sigh. Witches.

"What do you want?" I asked Zeke.

"I should think that's obvious. Though, looks like they killed the vampire we need."

"Yeah. And Aria's dead, too. Died in a fire."

"I doubt that."

"It's true. Your girl died, too. Hybrids set the cabin on fire."

"And how did you manage to escape? Lolly just told you about the trap door before she went up into flames?" Zeke cocked an eyebrow. "You're a terrible liar."

"Either way, they're gone."

"On the contrary. You must think we're really dumb. Or you somehow really trusted Lolly to get you all back to safety. We placed tracking serums inside you. We know where Lolly is, and we knew your every move. What we couldn't figure out is why you stayed nearby when they left. But I see, it's become abundantly clear. You're in love with a vampire, who's now dead."

"I never loved him."

"Sure. Well, we still need your blood."

I looked up, challenging him. "You want my blood? Come and get it." I darted toward the hybrids. No matter what I did, I would die. At least I'd get to see Alaric's face one more time.

Just as I reached the tail end of the hybrids, I felt strings or netting collapse over me, halting me in my tracks. I couldn't see the net, but it held me from moving further. I called Alaric's name, but it was as if I was alone in the forest.

Zeke walked up behind me. "Silly demon. Don't you know no one can hear you? You may be a demon, but I'm a witch and I'm much more powerful than you'll ever be. Come along. They're waiting for us."

As he walked away, the netting around me jerked in his direction as if he were pulling me along. He'd tethered us together with his magic. Whatever happened to him, would happen to me. Wherever he went, I went, too. No matter how much I fought against it, I was being dragged to my death.

I didn't understand how the witches could still perform the spell with only me. Even if they had found Aria, they needed three components. However, Caleb was a royal vampire as well. And Dmitry, Aria, and Lolly were headed straight there.

Dmitry would be so disappointed in me. As a Dominus member, and as someone who had been tortured for months, I needed to get out of this. I would not let the witches kill me before I sought revenge on Grayson. I needed to figure out a way to let Zeke release me from his magical tether. There had to be a way for me to escape the invisible chains. I was a demon. I was so much stronger than a witch.

"Zeke, wait," I said, trying out my innocent pleading voice.

He turned around, cocking that eyebrow. "What?"

"You want all three of us for your spell, right?"

"Yes."

"Even if Alaric is dead, you can still use his blood."

"Not if he's a shriveled-up vampire."

"What if he's not?"

"You want me to help you save him?"

"You're going to kill us anyway for a good cause. Would you at least do me the honor of seeing him one last time? I'll lead you to Aria."

"Thought she was dead?"

"You would want the same if it was someone you loved."

"I highly doubt a demon would ever grant me that kindness."

"I would."

He stared at me, contemplating. "You aren't lying."

"I'm not the monster you think I am. I know we were bred strictly for sport, but we've evolved."

Zeke let out a sigh. "I guess two is better than one for the spell. We aren't going to full on attack the hybrids. I have an invisibility spell placed on us. They can't see or hear us. We get in, grab the vampire, and get out."

"Okay. Will you release me from your tether?"

"No. We're in this together, remember?"

It was worth a shot, but I hoped he would give me enough range to take Alaric from the hybrids. It wouldn't be easy, but with a witch on my side, maybe he would see we were worth saving.

CHAPTER THIRTY-ONE
HARLOW

Zeke and I were invisible to the hybrids, but not to the raging snowstorm that brewed in the tempestuous midnight sky. Our invisibility also didn't erase our tracks in the snow, but we kept moving forward.

"If you cloaked the entire city, the hybrids won't see it at all?" I asked, making small talk, but also trying to gather information.

"That's what cloaking means."

"Why wasn't it cloaked the night Alaric brought me there?"

"Because we knew you were coming. We told Aria and Dmitry that the witches wanted her, and since Lolly is her best friend, we convinced her to make Aria come. We got lucky when you two showed up, but what I still can't understand is what delayed Aria and Dmitry?"

"They could've been attacked. How does this ritual go, exactly?"

"We sit you in a room and drain your blood. It's a simple process, just time consuming. We need all three of you and to start it at the same time, that way when you're all drained and the last drop is bled, you die, and we begin our chant."

Except that wouldn't happen. I was determined of that.

Rounding a corner, I saw the group of hybrids, still dragging Alaric's lifeless body. The demon in me rose. Anger built, and nothing would stop me. I sank into the snow and Zeke followed. "I need you to let me go so I can grab him. I'm faster than you."

"I'm not letting you go."

"As soon as I grab him, then you can reattach me to your chains. I have to be quick."

"And if I let you go, you will be exposed."

"We can't exactly sneak up on them."

"There's a goddamn blizzard going on right now. They won't notice a thing."

"Except as we're running away."

"Leave that part to me." Zeke's lips curled into a menacing smile.

I had no more time to argue. We crept up behind the hybrids, and with being invisible, I blended in with the group until I reached Alaric. Zeke followed, making sure no one touched us. Hoping they couldn't smell us or hear our racing heartbeats, I reached for Alaric's body, and suddenly there was a flash in the sky followed by a deafening crack. The blast knocked all the hybrids off their feet, and I seized Alaric's body.

Zeke and I fled from the hybrids, but not fast enough for me. We charged through the forest as I held my dead love in my arms. We had six hours before the sun rose that would turn Alaric's body to ash.

Once we were far enough away, we slowed our pace, but still ran. My heartbeat throbbed in my ears, but I heard a third beat. Distant, soft, and slow. I looked down at Alaric. He hadn't shriveled up. Leaning down to his face, I heard his heartbeat. He was alive.

Alaric needed to feed. He needed to heal. And the only thing near us that had blood was Zeke.

Dropping Alaric in the snow, I rushed up to Zeke and seized his head. With everything I had, I pulled his head from his body. The sound of flesh ripping apart was music to my ears. The cracking of his bones and the smell of blood as it exploded over me and the snow empowered me. His body collapsed with a thud and the chains disappeared. I brought his bleeding body to Alaric, letting his lips touch the blood.

I forced his mouth open, giving him a taste. For several seconds, I waited. He moved, and soon his fangs latched onto the skin and he began to drink.

Relief overcame me.

As Zeke's life left his body, I consumed his energy. I didn't care if it made me crazy, and I briefly wondered if I would have any witch powers. I watched Alaric drink in all the blood he needed. The demon in me wanted more power, especially since we were on the run.

Alaric moaned like he consumed the best meal of his life, and once he finished, he wiped his mouth. "You killed a witch for me?"

"Not at all. He tethered me to him. I don't like being restricted."

"You saved me from the hybrids."

"Maybe. Only because I didn't like the way they were dragging you along."

He smirked. "I'm sorry I left like I did."

"You'll make it up to me."

I couldn't hold back the demon any longer. I pounced on Alaric, kissing him. He kissed back, and I knew he was low on energy. I pulled away. "I'm sorry. It's the demon."

"It's okay, Harlow. I need to be close to you."

I rushed to remove his pants, just enough, and removed mine. I sank over his hardening cock and let out a sigh. I needed to be close to him, too. He was like a drug and I loved feeling him inside me. And if we were going to die, feeling his love for me one last time made it all worth it.

CHAPTER THIRTY-TWO
ALARIC

Making love to a beautiful woman in the middle of a blizzard had never happened to Alaric before, but there was always a first time for everything. This woman had saved him from the hybrids and killed a witch for him. Killing witches usually meant entire covens avenging their fallen soldier, but he'd protect Harlow with everything he had.

As she rode him, he stared up at her, loving the way her face contorted and the moans she made. He wasn't as energetic as her, but he knew she needed the power, and he would give her whatever she needed. Alaric watched her grind him and he reached down, pressing his thumb against her clit. He wouldn't be able to come this time, but he wanted to make sure she did. Harlow gasped and bit her lip. She picked up her pace and soon let out a cry.

Alaric sat up, wrapping his arms around her, and kissed her. "I promise I'll be better next time. I have a lot of making up to do."

"I never thought I would see you again."

"It's okay. I'm here."

"We need to go. We have to find the others."

"Where are they?" he asked as they untangled from each other and dressed.

"I told them to go ahead and that I would stay here."

"Couldn't stay away from me, I see," he said.

"I told you before. The sex is amazing and convenient," she teased.

Even through the banter, he was taken back by her commitment to him. Sure, they had expressed their love for each other, but so had he and Danielle, and that didn't turn out well. He had never expected to find love again, especially from a demon, but it seemed to come naturally from Harlow. He guessed after all those times of being tortured by vampires, she never learned to love. It wasn't easy, that was for sure, but it was definitely worth it, if the love was returned.

They trudged through the snow, exhausted, and ready to find a place called home. He wasn't sure what they could do to end the war without them dying, but he would figure something out.

"What did they do to you?" Harlow asked. "I saw Trajan dragging you. You looked so lifeless."

Alaric took her hand in his. It was such a human thing to do, and even though it had been years since he was a human, he still remembered bits of it, and he wanted to comfort her somehow. "Trajan shot me with one those damn demon guns making my blood harden."

My hands clenched into fists. "I swear, I'm going to kill him next time I see him."

"He's sired to Grayson, Harlow."

"What? How is that possible?"

"He said it was because of his blood. He also said the hybrids are forced to protect Grayson at all costs, no matter what. And that if Grayson dies the hybrids die along with him."

"How did Trajan even find Grayson and join him? He's been a hybrid for a few months now."

"I have no idea. We didn't talk much."

"He just left Danielle like that?"

"Sounds like it." He didn't understand it either, but he didn't care enough to find out since Trajan fought with him and shot him.

"He's just completely turned on us. He shouldn't have shot you. Do you think Grayson forced him to?"

"I don't know. Grayson mentioned wanting to turn me into a hybrid."

"You were going to die, Alaric. They were going to parade you around in front of the witches. What are we going to do?"

"We'll figure it out." He squeezed her hand again. "Everything will be okay. Danielle, Caleb and the others will have found an army." At least he hoped they had. Something had to give them hope, and lately not much of that was going around.

As they walked hand in hand, the snowstorm finally calmed down to a light snow. He still kept an ear out for hybrids and witches.

"How did you become a vampire?" she asked, and he hadn't thought about that in so long. It was a past life and sometimes he forgot what it was like to be a human.

"It was so long ago. There was a plague going on and yours truly got it. There was a doctor of sorts who kept claiming he had a cure for it, but it was costly. He didn't want money, he just wanted to use us as his experiments. He didn't care about us. Hundreds of people died, but we were unaware that his "cure" was actually vampirism. He was using vampire blood, and well, I woke up with a burning in my throat and a hunger I had never felt before."

"That sounds awful. Why do people think we're science experiments? And demons tortured you, too."

"They did." He didn't like talking about it, but telling Harlow was okay. She was curious and wanted to know more.

"I hated vampires, until I met you. You're different."

"I feel the same about you. You make me want to be a better person."

"You aren't bad, Alaric. You've had a lot of bad shit happen to you, same as me. You've made me feel things I never thought were possible. And you don't think I'm a monster."

"You aren't."

"Neither are you."

When they came up to a lone highway in the middle of the mountain, Harlow turned to him, gazing at him like she was in love. It took a few minutes for them to tear their eyes away. She moved toward the road and lay down.

"What are you doing?" he asked.

"Lie down next to me."

Another reason Harlow didn't bother him, was that he trusted her and knew she would do anything to save him.

"Okay."

"Just close your eyes and wait."

They lay next to each other, listening to their quiet breathing. He could hear Harlow's pounding heartbeat, and it made him smirk. He loved that he made her feel that way. He did something that caught himself off guard again. He took her hand in his and intertwined their fingers. He surprised himself with the things he did with Harlow.

In the midst of all the hell, she'd been his saving grace. She'd kept him from completely losing it, multiple times. She let him fall apart and didn't run. Which was more than he could say for himself. She never judged him, and she let him be himself in ways he had never been with anyone. He didn't do love or relationships, but damn if Harlow hadn't changed that thought process for him.

Alaric had fallen in love with a demon. Something he never thought he could manage, since most of his life had been spent killing them. She was so easy to be around and to talk to. With everything going on, she was the star brightening his sky.

Rolling his eyes behind his closed lids, he thought of how ridiculous his thoughts sounded. He could feel part of his old human self emerging.

Finally, a car rumbled down the road and screeched to a halt.

Alaric gave a quiet chuckle.

The car door opened, and the humans emerged from the car in a frantic motion.

"Omigod, are you okay?" a young woman asked as she stood over them. She smelled sweet and Alaric was salivating. He knew Harlow had never killed an innocent human until recently, but he loved that she took his advice and realized that no one was truly innocent.

When Harlow opened her eyes, the woman gasped. He knew she saw her red eyes and he smiled. The fear in her eyes excited Alaric, and Harlow grabbed her and tore off her arm in a symphony of sounds. Her scream was the most powerful and he saw Harlow thrive on it. Demons could never be clean with their killing, and it used to annoy him, but watching Harlow tear apart a human like it was a rag doll amazed him.

Alaric quickly captured the passenger and fed on him. While the girl lay frozen in fear, Harlow took all of her life energy and joined Alaric as he drained the man of blood. He watched her inhale the man's life and reveled in her joy. The surge of energy lifted him. Once they were through with the man, they finished off the woman.

"Wanna go for a ride?" Alaric smiled and held open the door to the Porsche for Harlow. She slid into the passenger seat, and Alaric got into the driver's side. He put it in gear and the car purred as they sped on the empty road in the cold night.

They had found their way to a mountain top that overlooked what used to be the city. It was darker now after

Grayson's army destroyed it all. Alaric missed the bustling city life. But even in the midst of the destruction, he'd found hope with Harlow. She definitely wasn't what he had expected especially for being a demon. But she made him happier than he had been. She made him feel emotions he had buried deep inside. She let him be himself and she was never afraid of him.

They had gotten out of the gasless Porsche, knowing they couldn't waste any more time getting back to the hideout.

Harlow lay back against the snowy ground and looked beautiful under the moon's glow. He memorized her features and loved each and every curve of her body. He lay next to her on his side and pressed his hand to her stomach, blithely moving her top up to touch her bare flesh. It gave him chills feeling her soft skin.

When his hand slipped further, she moaned and moved with him. He quickly unbuttoned her jeans and slipped his hand inside. When he pushed two fingers inside her warmth, she gasped and spread her legs wide. Alaric wanted to taste her, and he loved being outside in the middle of nowhere making Harlow feel good. He never wanted to say goodbye to her again and refused to let anything come between them.

CHAPTER THIRTY-THREE
HARLOW

Fire tore through my body as Alaric's face was in my pussy. I moaned as he licked and sucked my clit harder. I grabbed a handful of his hair and pulled it. He knew exactly what to do as always. He was the only one who made me feel this good, so alive. He made me feel loved and wasn't afraid of me. He let me be myself.

My body burned with desire as I climbed higher to reach that point, and once I came, he met me with kisses and pushed his hard cock inside me. Thrusting hard, it felt so good I forgot to breathe. I loved feeling him inside me, so full, so complete. He filled my heart and gave me a powerful confidence. He made me feel so sexy and beautiful. I would do anything for him, and I did.

We had no time to waste, but I needed him in that moment. Being apart from him almost killed me and I refused to be apart from him again. If we were going to die in a war, I'd rather be by his side. If we had no way out of the war alive, I wanted as many moments with him as we could get.

Alaric pumped inside me as he held my legs up around his waist. He gazed at me as he continued his steady rhythm. Pressing his thumb against my clit, he moved it with vigor.

"Let go, Harlow. Tell me how good I make you feel."

I pushed up on my elbows and watched his hard cock move in and out of me. It was incredibly hot. "Bite me, Alaric."

He pulled out and turned me around so that my back was against his chest. He eased his cock inside me and I grinded against him. Moving my hair aside, I heard his fangs extend. He slapped my clit at the same time his teeth sank into my neck. I moved faster against him as he rubbed my clit with the same speed. Licking his bite mark, I cried out as the orgasm crashed throughout me.

Alaric pushed me onto my hands and knees and fucked me hard until he came inside me.

"You feel so goddamn good," he said. "I love you, Harlow."

"I love you."

"I wanna be inside you forever."

I wanted that, too, and maybe we would have that once the war was over.

We dressed and began making our way back to the hideout. I hadn't seen Dmitry or Aria or anyone and hoped we would find them.

The sky had a light purple hue and melted into orange. We didn't have much time before the sun would rise. Alaric and I needed to hurry back to the cabin. I knew the witches had a tracker on me, but so had Lolly. We just needed to get in and get out. Follow Grayson and kill him. I didn't care if it would kill Trajan. I was a demon and I was determined to win this war.

"We need to hurry," I told him.

"I know."

"Maybe we can find another car and you can hide in the trunk," I told Alaric.

"We'll make it."

"Do you think they found an army?" I asked.

"I hope they did. I don't know how they found Trajan or if he just left. I'm not entirely sure how siring works."

As we walked, something didn't feel right. I looked around and saw nothing. The demon in me rose, knowing someone was watching us. Had they seen us make love? I couldn't smell anything.

"What is it?" he asked.

"You don't feel that?"

"Feels like someone's following us."

"We need a car."

Alaric grabbed my hand and led me down the mountain. We ran, ignoring the rocks and bare tree branches. We heard voices around us. I didn't want to be afraid, but I was.

We came to a clearing, and once I saw the sun barely crest above the horizon, my heart sprung. There was no cover. We couldn't go back.

"Fuck. Come on, maybe there's a bunker or something," Alaric said.

We picked up our pace and ran, but as we trudged through the clearing, there was a line of people waiting for us. Alaric stopped me, pulling me behind him. He protected me still even though we were both fucked.

"No matter what happens—"

"Don't say any of that mushy shit right now."

"Just think of my naked body and how much you like it."

I let out a laugh. We were about to be taken hostage or killed and Alaric could still make me laugh.

Soon, the group of people surrounded us. No one said a word. They were all calm, and I couldn't hear a single heartbeat. Witches.

Then Ciara appeared from the group. "Going somewhere?"

"Trying to," I said.

"You've escaped our grasp one too many times. We still need your blood and it appears this is the only way to achieve that." She raised a gun and fired.

A bullet went straight to Alaric's chest and he fell to his knees.

Fuck.

"Alaric," I yelled, but as I lunged for him, she fired again and like slow motion, the bullet slammed into my chest. It wasn't a bullet the demons created. Or vampires. Something strange was happening. I felt paralyzed, yet I could still move. Falling to my knees, I seized my chest as searing pain shot through me.

"Alaric," I struggled to say. He grabbed my hand and pulled me to him.

As we collapsed in the snow, we stared at each other. I was fading, and everything became blurry until I saw nothing else.

CHAPTER THIRTY-FOUR
HARLOW

When I woke, I felt no better. My arms ached, and I shivered. I had no energy at all, and as I looked around, there was a simple light by what looked like a door. The sweet metallic smell of blood overwhelmed me forcing nausea to flitter around in my stomach. Strange. I always loved the smell of blood. It hungered the demon.

I tried moving, but my body was pinned down and everything felt like a hundred pounds. Lifting my head, I realized I was restrained to a steel table, just like when the vampires experimented on me. Next to me was Alaric strapped down onto a table. Tubes and needles attached to our arms sucking our blood into fucking buckets. The goddamn witches were draining us of our blood. If our blood was that sacred, it seemed like they could've used something else other than a plastic bucket. But something else was off. I didn't feel powerful. Something was missing, like a part of me was gone. I didn't understand it.

"Alaric," I said, as my throat felt like I had swallowed razors. "Alaric."

He moaned as he slowly opened his eyes. Those beautiful green eyes trained on me, and once he comprehended what was happening, he struggled against his restraints. "What the fuck is this? I can hardly move. What did they give us?"

"I don't know."

I wasn't scared when Grayson came to the Lair with his machismo ultimatum and had his hybrids blow up the place. I wasn't scared when vampires held me hostage and pricked and prodded me until their heart's desire. But fear crept inside me and latched on for dear life. It gripped me and bled through my eyes. What was going on? I was a demon. Demons didn't fear, and if they did it was never so strong or intense.

"Harlow?" Alaric asked. "Are you okay?"

Tears poured out of my eyes, and I couldn't answer him. I heard him struggling against his restraints again and I finally forced myself to stop crying. I don't remember ever feeling like that. What the fuck was wrong with me? Maybe that was what happened when all your blood drained from your body.

"Alaric, I'm so dizzy and I want to throw up."

"I know. Me too. I can't even grow my fangs. It's like they gave us something to prevent us from regenerating."

"Is that why I feel pain all over?"

"Yeah."

"Vampires never did this to me. They at least let me rest."

"Same with demons," Alaric said.

"What do we do? We can't die like this."

"We won't."

The door swung open and Ciara walked in with her witch friend. "Looks like they're almost done," Ciara said.

"What did you do to us?" Alaric demanded.

"Not so tough, now are you?"

"I swear I will rip your fucking head off," I threatened.

Ciara laughed. "Even if I let you go right now, you would barely be able to walk. This was the only way to take your blood."

"What did you shoot us with?" Alaric asked.

"Just a little something we whipped up. So many of your kind will be so thrilled about it. I told you we had plans for you all. Vampires and demons should not exist. And they won't."

"Why do you have to punish them all by killing off the entire species? It wasn't our fault we became like this."

"No, but you did choose this life. However, you're correct. The species will die, but in its place will be humans as you should be."

"What?"

"I wish you two could enjoy it while it lasted, but that's the sacrifice you have to make."

"What are you talking about?" I asked. I was tired of her mumbo jumbo and my head was too fuzzy to figure it out.

"My dear child. You're both humans. We concocted a cure to vampirism and demonism. Once the hybrids and Grayson are dead, we will begin dispersing the cure in the water supply of humans, in every way they consume so that when a vampire bites into a human, they'll be cured. Or when a demon rips apart a human, their blood will seep into the demons' bloodstream, curing them. It's unfortunate that some humans may have to be sacrificed in order for it to happen, but it's for the best."

I couldn't believe what I heard. Witches had created a cure. There was no way. There had never been a cure or whatever to vampirism or demonism. But it made sense. Witches created both species. And now they were destroying everything they had created.

CHAPTER THIRTY-FIVE
ALARIC

Alaric's head was so distorted that nothing the witch said made sense. There was no way in hell witches could end vampirism like that. If the witches were going to clean them out, at least they could let Alaric and Harlow hold each other.

Fuck.

He couldn't remember the last time he felt that shitty. He was in and out of consciousness and every time he woke up, he wanted to puke. Someone tugged on his restraints and he moaned as he opened his eyes. A figure with dark hair stood over him.

"Alaric wake up." He recognized the voice, but it was garbled and faint. He couldn't see Harlow on the other table. Alaric wanted to struggle against whoever made him sit up. He wanted Harlow. He needed her.

The person helped Alaric out of the room and down a hallway. He heard several hushed voices, but none of them were Harlow.

The walls melted, and his legs were worthless. It felt like he was walking on an unstable bridge. Everything spun, no matter how hard he tried to concentrate on stopping it. It almost felt like he was floating. He tried so hard to keep his eyes open or to at least make an effort to walk, but it was useless.

Alaric threw up and lost consciousness again.

"Alaric wake up." Someone kept shouting as they shoved something across his mouth. "Drink. You need to drink so you can heal."

A warm liquid dripped into his mouth, and at first, he almost gagged from the metallic taste, but he drank anyway. It tasted like blood, which he needed to feed. He couldn't remember the last time he fed. Within minutes, he felt better, refreshed. He was tired, but he didn't feel like death was knocking.

Alaric opened his eyes and saw Danielle leaning over him. "Oh, I'm so glad you're okay. I was so worried." Relief showed in her brown eyes. She was beautiful, more than he remembered. It was like he was seeing her for the first time. Her skin seemed to present a faint glow or maybe he was still fucked up from whatever the witches had done.

"What's going on? Where is Harlow?"

"She's safe."

"Where is she?" Alaric sat up and tried ignoring the dizziness. "Fuck. What is wrong with me?"

"You don't remember, do you?"

"Everything is a blur. Witches were draining our blood."

Scanning the room, he recognized it. He was back at the hideout. They needed to get out of there since the witches could track Harlow and Lolly. As if on cue, his door opened and Lolly appeared. Her auburn hair fell in messy curls and she looked like she hadn't slept in days.

"I just came to see if you're okay."

"I'm fine."

Lolly ran to him, wrapping her arms around him. His head ached, and he wanted her off of him. "I was so worried about you."

"Yeah." He'd forgotten he made her think he was in love with her. He needed to compel her. "I'm sorry." He removed her arms from his neck and stared into her eyes. "You need to forget about me. We aren't lovers."

She stepped back, furrowing her eyebrows. "Forget about you? It isn't that simple. I've been sick for days thinking you died."

His compulsion hadn't worked. The witches really must have done a number on him. But he just drank blood, so why hadn't it worked? He shook his head. Witches must have given her something to protect against it. But she'd been with Danielle for days or even weeks or however long he and Harlow had been gone. It should have left her system by now. "Why can't you be compelled?"

"You tried to compel me?" Lolly asked, offended. "Why would you do that?"

Danielle bit her lip. "Alaric, you can't compel anyone."

"What? Did the witches weaken me that much?"

Danielle hesitated. "You're human, Alaric."

Her words hung in the air like his mind refused to comprehend. But the more he focused on them, it brought back the conversation with the maniacal witch, Ciara. Witches had found a way to turn vampires back to humans. He couldn't decide if being human was worse than death.

Lolly gasped and stepped back as if he was suddenly diseased. "What? He's a-a human?"

"How is that even possible?" Alaric asked.

Danielle shrugged. "Witches found a way."

"Are they dead?"

"A lot of them are."

"Where's Harlow? I need to see her."

"She's resting in the other room," Lolly said. "Why do you care?"

Alaric didn't have time to deal with petty shit. He stood from the bed, ignoring the dizziness, and forced his way to Harlow's room. When he opened her door, she turned to face him, and his heart skipped a beat. Seeing her standing there, looking so vulnerable, and gorgeous, made his body relax with relief, but it thrilled him. Her skin looked incredibly soft and her blond hair reached her shoulders.

"Alaric." They met halfway in an embrace, and he held onto her as tight as he could, loving the sweet jasmine scent of her. He didn't think he would ever see her again, or that they would be alive.

"I can't believe we got out of that," she said. "How did they know where to find us?"

"Lolly and Elijah knew where you'd be," Danielle said from behind them.

Still holding onto Harlow, Alaric turned to face the door. "Who's Elijah?"

Danielle sighed. "It's a long story."

"Zeke's brother," Lolly said as she appeared next to Danielle. "He's helping us out. He helped us rescue you two."

Harlow stiffened. She had killed Zeke for Alaric and he drank his blood. "No. I killed Zeke. He's only here for revenge. Witches almost killed us. We have to get out of here," she said, panic in her voice. "The witches put tracking serums in me and Lolly. That's how he found us."

"You killed Zeke?" Lolly gasped. "Why would you do that? You really are a monster."

"He was taking us back to the witches. I had no choice, and Alaric was unconscious."

Her expression softened knowing that her killing Zeke saved Alaric, but then she glared at Harlow. "Well, for your information, I never drank the witch's potion. I knew what they were doing to me. They can't find us here. But I see my helping you was all a lie."

"Would you have helped us otherwise?" Harlow asked.

"Yes. I wanted out of there badly. Elijah only wants to help us."

"Why would he help us? What's in it for him? Where is he?" She pushed through Danielle and Lolly and Alaric followed her downstairs and into the main room. When she found Elijah, she walked right up to him. "Are you lying? Why are you helping us?"

"I'm not lying," he said, sincerely. He wasn't scared or arrogant like Zeke had been. He stood nonchalantly as if he knew he needed to be interrogated a thousand times before anyone would believe him. Alaric had tried to be that patient before with the group, and he admired Elijah's patience.

"I have reasons for helping, but I'd rather not say out loud," he said, and Alaric didn't miss him throw a glance in Lolly's direction. "You can trust me."

"I killed your brother, and I'm not afraid to kill you if I have to."

"I know he's dead."

Harlow stared at him for a moment and let out a frustrated sigh. "I'm too weak to detect lying."

"It's okay, Harlow," Dmitry said. "We've already talked to him. We've all decided he's one of us."

"Don't you think this is something the Dominus should have discussed and decided?"

Fuck.

She didn't know.

Dmitry cleared his throat and moved toward her. "We did."

"Okay, where was I?"

Sawyer and Mina flanked Dmitry and she stared at them.

"You just kicked me out of the Dominus? I didn't die. Once I get my strength back, I'll be fine."

Everyone in the room frowned and looked away, except Dmitry and Alaric.

"Harlow, you're not a demon," Dmitry said. "You're a human."

She gasped and swayed slightly. "No. No it was just a dream. The witches made me think that. It's not true though." She turned back to Alaric with sadness and fear in her brown eyes.

"It's true," he said, hating himself for having to agree. "We're both human." He wanted to comfort her, but he knew she needed time to process all of it. He needed time to process it, too.

Her face fell, and Alaric knew exactly how she felt. That everything would change and that the transition wouldn't be easy. The invincibility, the power, all of it was gone. In some ways it felt like they might as well have been dead because what was their purpose now? Would they even belong to the group anymore or have to figure out life on their own?

"Can you become a demon and vampire again?" Aria asked.

"I don't know," Alaric said. "The witches didn't exactly give us a handbook on this."

Harlow turned back to Elijah. "We'll just turn back once we have our strength."

Sawyer ran his hand through his red hair. "I'm afraid you can't."

"Why not?" she demanded.

Alaric urged Elijah to explain. Might as well get all of the truth out now rather than later.

"If you ingest demon energy or a vampire bites either of you, you'll die."

"What? We have vampire blood inside us," Alaric said.

"And you should be careful until it leaves your system."

"What the fuck?" she screamed. "You're going to believe him? Of course, he'll make you believe anything. That's what witches do. He's enchanted every one of you. He's going to turn against us."

"Harlow, he's clean," Sawyer said.

"But we have magical blood or whatever. That's why the witches wanted us. We have immortal blood."

"It's gone. Once the witches shot you with their serum, it made your bodies slowly transition to humans. They collected all of your magical blood, but since you didn't die, they can't do the spell. But they'll try something again."

Alaric moved behind Harlow and she fell into him. "What happened to Trajan?"

Danielle's eyes zeroed in on Alaric in an intense glare. He felt a little fearful now that he was human, and he definitely couldn't fight her off anymore. "He left us." She turned for the staircase, and as much as he wanted to keep his mouth shut, he didn't.

"He's sired to Grayson."

She froze and twisted her head. "What?"

"All of the hybrids are sired to him." He looked at Sawyer. "Caroline is with them, too."

He closed his eyes and Danielle's face fell, but she regained some hope in her brown eyes. "You two should rest. You don't exactly have the stamina anymore. We'll reconvene tonight."

Alaric tugged Harlow as they followed Danielle upstairs and went into Harlow's room, closing the door.

She was more beautiful, and her brown eyes were soft and kind. He would miss that sexy ruby color, but as long as he still had her in his life, that was all that mattered.

Touching her face and skin felt different, like a thousand shocks circulating all over his body. He grabbed his chest once he felt the constant pounding. He never thought he would ever hear that again. Harlow pressed her hand to his and smiled.

"It's beating so fast."

"That's what you do to me."

Cradling her face, he leaned down and pressed his lips to hers. His heart exploded into an erratic rhythm as their tongues tangled. He didn't rush through it, and neither did she. Harlow pulled him closer until they were on the bed with him on top. He wanted to make love, but he was still exhausted.

She kissed him softly and after they situated themselves under the blankets, Harlow drew back. "Will you please stay here tonight? I can't get rid of this overwhelming fear."

"Of course." He wrapped his arms tightly around her. "I'm not going anywhere."

They lay like that until they fell asleep.

CHAPTER THIRTY-SIX
HARLOW

Blood drained out of my arm like it was a water faucet. The queasy feeling washed over me. The blood wouldn't stop. Fear gripped me as I watched it flood into a bucket. Witches laughed, knowing I couldn't move. Bombs exploded as Grayson casually walked away.

My eyes bolted open and I gasped. Sweat covered me as my heart pounded like it would shoot through my chest. I had to have died in that explosion. That was the only explanation to how shitty I felt. Scanning the room, I realized I was at the hideout, and my eyes landed on Alaric sitting in the chair watching the sun. Gazing at him, I no longer felt hatred for him. He was no longer a vampire. I wasn't a demon. We were the same. The passion was still there, and while we were safe for however long, I wanted to make the best of it.

When he saw me staring, he stood from the chair. He closed the distance, the air around us felt like we stood next to a volcano. My heart beat, stopped, then beat again. Alaric stared into my eyes with full lust. I couldn't breathe properly as he swept my hair aside and left his hand lingering on my cheek. Lowering his lips, he softly pressed them to mine. He cradled my head in his hands and slipped his tongue inside. For a second, I imagined his tongue licking my clit. I wanted him, and when he pressed his body against mine, I could tell he wanted me. He fisted my hair and kissed me harder, moaning into my mouth.

Alaric slipped his hand under my shirt and his touch sent tingles throughout me. I wanted to touch him, run my hands on his chest. He undressed and moved on top of me on the bed.

His cock hardened against my leg as I deepened the kiss. Searing heat filled my entire body and I ached for him. Alaric removed my shirt, and once his mouth latched onto my nipple, I gasped. Everything felt so new, so strong, so intense. He reached down and pressed his fingers against my clit and pushed them inside my pussy. He pumped his fingers a few times. It felt different, but a good different. It was as if we needed to make it last, like it was our first time.

"I'm sorry. I need to be inside you." He spat on his hand and rubbed it on himself before pushing inside me. I wasn't instantly wet, but after a few strokes, he glided in and out of me with ease. His cock felt bigger as it filled me completely. "Fuck. You feel amazing."

I couldn't think. He made me feel so good that every inch of me was encased in his love. He thrust in and out at a steady pace until he slowed down, and I felt him throb.

"You feel amazing." He kissed me. "You didn't come did you?"

"No, but it still felt great. We can always try again later."

He smiled. "It's different. A good different."

"I know what you mean."

We dressed and met everyone in the main room. It felt different being around them, but at the same time it didn't. Sawyer handed us both a shot of whiskey and I downed mine, but immediately felt nauseous.

"Oh. There's food in the refrigerator," Lolly said. "You guys are probably hungry."

Harlow hadn't needed food to sustain herself in years. That was definitely going to take some getting used to.

Dmitry let out a frustrated sigh. "I can't believe this has happened."

I laughed. Apparently, being human gave me zero tolerance to alcohol.

"It's definitely not ideal," Alaric said. "But I'm not alone." He squeezed my hand.

"How is it even possible?" Sawyer asked.

"Witches have been working on a concoction to end vampirism and demonism," Elijah said.

"That was their plan? They weren't going to kill anyone? Just have people inadvertently drink the elixir so that when vampires and demons killed them, they would ingest it and turn to human."

"That's exactly it," Elijah said."

I remembered some of what Ciara told us, but it was still a blur.

"Trajan's sired to Grayson," Alaric said. "If we kill Grayson, all of the hybrids die, including Trajan and Caroline."

"Well that's not an option," Danielle said.

The witches had come up with a way to change vampires and demons into humans, and Grayson was a vampire. He wasn't a hybrid. "What if we gave Grayson the cure?" I looked at Alaric. "He wouldn't die. The hybrids would still be alive and wouldn't be sired."

"That could work," Dmitry said.

"We need to get the army ready. We need to figure out a way to stop the witches. They want to cure the entire races."

"What?"

"Yeah. We should get a group together and invade—"

"Harlow," Dmitry said.

"What?"

"You aren't in charge anymore. You're not a Dominus member."

His words hit me, and a heaviness sank in my stomach. I was no longer a Dominus member. I couldn't swallow the bulge that lodged in my throat. My heart pounded, and I couldn't control my breathing.

"We can still help," I demanded, trying to cover up my emotions. How had humans done it?

"Harlow, it's too dangerous now."

"You and I are the same now," Lolly said and I wanted to throat punch her.

"Think about it. Witches can't do anything to us. We can get you inside that place and get the cure."

Lolly scoffed. "I think they got in there just fine to save you two."

I lunged for her throat and squeezed. "One more word out of you and I will break your neck."

Alaric pulled me off her. "Harlow's right. They won't be expecting us to come back. We can do this. Let us do this."

Dmitry contemplated our words. Sawyer and Mina stood next to him. Caleb and Danielle were on the couch with Estrella and London.

"How do we know it will break the sire bond?" Danielle asked.

"We don't, but you would rather he die?" Alaric asked.

"His hybrid army has diminished quite a bit since we convinced the races to join us, but now we need to figure out how to fight the witches," Caleb said. "What if we burn their spell books?"

"If they can be destroyed," Mina said.

"If not, we can always hide them. I assume you know where they keep them." Caleb looked at Elijah.

Lolly sighed. "You think we're really going to help you after that psycho tried to kill me?"

"She won't kill you," Alaric said. "She's been through a lot and she's frustrated."

"We've all been through a lot."

Caleb moved closer to Elijah. "You have any ideas?"

"Grimoires cannot be destroyed," he said. "However, we can take them somewhere and spellbind the place to where only the witch who placed the spell can get inside."

"Meaning you?" Mina asked, and I knew she doubted his plan. It seemed a little too easy for me. If this witch wanted to rule, that would be his plan.

"Yes. But I promise I'm on your side. After I put them inside a vault, and place a spell, one of you vampires can compel me to forget."

"Unless you can fight of the compulsion."

"For fucks sake, he's not lying," Lolly shouted. "He just saved two of you and you're all still in disbelief."

"Excuse us for feeling that way," I said. "We were almost killed by fucking witches and they made us humans."

"At least you're still alive," she pointed out. "You should be thankful for that. Besides, being a human isn't as bad as you seem to think."

"Is that why you want to be a part of this world? Because being a human is boring and you want more?"

"My life hasn't been easy. It's just an escape."

"You think my life has been a breeze?"

"Please. You got everything you ever wanted."

I curled my hands into fists, and Alaric held me back. Lolly knew nothing about me or what I was going through or what all I had been through.

"Lolly, Elijah, will you please help us," Aria pleaded. "This is the only way we can go about doing this without so much bloodshed."

"Only if I get to help, too."

"Jesus fuck! What is it with you all?" Caleb cursed. "You're all humans which could slow us down and you may not be able to do as much as you once did. Do you know how difficult it's going to be to get through the witches, steal the potions, spell books, then fight the hybrids to even get to Grayson?"

"Yeah, we get it," I told him. "But this is still our war. Whether we're humans or not. We still belong here. And we have a witch on our side to help out."

Dmitry, Mina, and Sawyer exchanged looks.

Dmitry sighed. "Fine."

"You're making a mistake by letting them help," Caleb said.

"Elijah can help us get the cure," I told him. "Witches won't know we're there because he can hide us."

Caleb rolled his eyes.

Mina seized his arm. "If they say they can do it, they can. Harlow and Alaric are smart. And human or not, they know how to fight."

"What about the grimoires?" Lolly asked.

"I have a satchel that can hold a lot," Elijah said.

Everyone looked at him like he was crazy.

"Trust me. It's magical."

"We need to feed and get the army ready," Caleb said, and as most of them made their way toward the door, a small part of me felt sad because I wasn't joining them.

After they left, it was just Lolly, Elijah, Alaric, and me. It was quiet, but my head was loud with thoughts. Lolly and Elijah prepared sandwiches for us and as much as I hated her, I appreciated the food.

"Would you want to change back?" Alaric asked once we were back in my room.

"Yes, but that won't ever happen. The witches have wreaked havoc all over my body lately. But there is one thing about being human that I like."

"What's that?"

"I don't feel any hatred toward you. I was so afraid our love was some trick by the witches, but it's real, isn't it?"

"Of course, it's real. I feel no hatred toward you either." Cradling my face between his hands, he pressed his lips to mine, kissing me like he never wanted to let me go. It was different than before. It held more meaning, and as much as I didn't want to admit it, Lolly was right. I should be thankful that we were still alive and that we had each other. And I was.

As our tongues tangled, we undressed each other, and he lifted me up and set me down on top of the table. Getting to his knees, he settled between my legs and my heart pounded with anticipation. The moment his tongue touched my clit, I sighed. Licking, sucking, and nibbling, he didn't stop until I cried out. He always made me feel incredible.

Lifting my legs, he held them under my knees as he slid his hard cock inside me. I whimpered as he filled me to the hilt. He started out slow as he watched us but picked up his pace. Watching him move and seeing his muscles contract made me hot. I was so in love with him. As his hot seed came inside me, he picked me up with him still inside, and brought me to the bed.

"I love you so much, Harlow. Always."

CHAPTER THIRTY-SEVEN
ALARIC

Peering out the window, Alaric stilled at the sight of the sun. With Harlow, naked, in his arms, being human had been hard, but wanting to know if he could feel the sun's warmth excited him. "I know you're tired, and it's probably cold outside, but I need to feel the sun again."

Harlow smiled. "I can't imagine what that must have been like."

"That was one of the things I missed most."

She untangled herself from him and they dressed.

Harlow groaned as she wrapped a scarf around her neck. "I hate having to wear all these clothes. They're too restricting."

"I know."

She followed him outside. He wasn't lying, it was cold, but once they reached the sunlight, he inhaled a deep breath.

The warmth of the sun heated his cold and battered body. He missed the simple pleasure, and he almost felt giddy. But when he turned to Harlow, the frown on her face almost killed him.

"Are you okay?"

Tears clouded her eyes and she shook her head. "No. None of this is okay. I'm weak. I'm cold. When Dmitry said I wasn't a Dominus member anymore, it did something to me. I feel like I've lost part of myself."

"I know. I feel it, too."

"I don't want to be a human, Alaric."

"I don't either, but it's better than the alternative."

Harlow sighed. "I know. I didn't mean to ruin your moment in the sun."

Alaric rolled his eyes. "You didn't. Maybe you got used to being a demon for so long that you don't know how to be a human. I know that's how I feel now."

"You do?"

"Of course. Yeah, feeling the sun again is amazing, but I'm not sure I'm meant to be a human."

"I feel that way, too. I feel lost. I don't even remember being human."

Alaric gathered her into his arms and held her. "I barely remember, but together we can do this. It's going to take time, but we're strong enough to get through anything." He cradled her face in his hands, forcing her to meet his gaze. "I wouldn't want to do this without you, Harlow."

She smiled, and he hadn't seen her smile that warmly since the transition. "What do you remember most about being human?"

"Memories are becoming more abundant, but I remember everything feeling so…lasting. How old were you when you became a demon?"

"Nineteen. I was so young, I barely remember that life. It was so long ago."

Alaric nodded.

"I've been a demon for so long. I used to be invincible. Strong. And so confident. Now, I don't know how to feel.

I don't know how to live. I'm so fucking emotional now," she said and wiped her eyes.

It was odd seeing her cry, and he didn't like it because there wasn't anything he could do. But he agreed with her. He felt so ordinary. It was odd not feeling so powerful and on top of the world. "Harlow, you're still strong. And confident. You haven't lost that, and you won't. When you became a demon, it only amplified those things, but you are who you've always been."

She shook her head. "No. As a human, I was a scared little girl who never took things seriously. I had always taken advantage of everything. Being a demon made me realize who I really was. It gave me a purpose. I felt like I belonged, and it was right. But maybe I felt that way because I wanted to kill vampires for what they did."

"I understand. But who you've been this whole time will stay with you."

"I don't feel like it. Fear is crippling me, like it always did before. When vampires killed my family, I feared they would come for me."

"I know it's hard. We don't have those certain traits that made us invincible, but now we have purpose. We have reason now. That was always something as a vampire I never felt like I had. A reason for living. What was the point? But I took advantage of it. And now we have a life that we can build."

He spoke like someone who had wanted to become a human for a while, and perhaps he had always thought about it deep down and ignored it. How long had he thought about it? He was so sure he loved being a vampire, and he had, but now as a human, it was as if he'd been given a second chance. A chance to make things right, to make it count. And with Harlow, he'd show her all the wonderful things about being a human.

CHAPTER THIRTY-EIGHT
HARLOW

The unforgiving bitter wind howled in the freezing black night. I hugged myself tighter. Wearing a scarf, a beanie, a thick coat still wasn't enough. Lolly had gone with others and gotten clothes for the pathetic humans. I hated it. I hated having to wear so many layers. But I loved feeling Alaric's warm hand grab mine. It made me feel like I wasn't alone, and that no matter what, he'd always be there.

I knew he was trying to help me earlier and make it sound like being a human wouldn't be bad, and it made me wonder if he had always wanted to return to his human life. He'd sounded like he'd thought about it for a while. Maybe he had, and as much as I didn't want to be a human, I had to learn again. Watching Alaric smile earlier as he basked in the sunlight made my heart warm. It was such a foreign feeling, something so long lost. I almost didn't know what to do with it.

As Alaric, Elijah, Lolly, and me made our way toward the witch's hideout, vampires and demons flanked us but miles away. The plan was for them to surround the hideout, but if the witches had placed a spell over it, I wasn't sure how anyone would be able to see it. Elijah assured us that invisibility spells didn't work against humans because they were immune. I guessed we'd find out for sure if we saw some random place in the middle of the woods.

No matter what happened, I wanted to prove myself that I still belonged to the group, that I was still a demon at heart or whatever that phrase was. That I still served a purpose.

We approached a building in the woods with no lights and it looked boarded up.

"You see the building?" Elijah asked.

"Yes," I said.

"That's what it looks like to humans. Demons and vampires can't see anything. It disappears for them."

"What happens if I go inside? Or if any human finds it and wants to seek shelter?"

"Then it will still appear as an abandoned shack. But walk closer and tell me what you feel."

I looked at him, confused, but took a few steps forward. Suddenly, I felt unsafe. It was like something bad was going to happen. Looking behind me, there wasn't a threat of danger, but I felt it deep to my core. "What are you doing to me?"

"Nothing. That's what the spell does. It spooks humans. The closer they get, the more amplified the feelings become."

"Fucking witches," Alaric said. "They always have all the tricks up their sleeves."

"We have to in order to survive against you—or who you used to be."

Alaric squeezed my hand and I knew, even in the dark, he winced. "Just do your magic so we can get this over with already."

Elijah held up his hands, and within seconds, the abandoned building turned into a dimly lit house that definitely didn't look abandoned. It appeared to be a warm and cozy house, but from what I remembered, it was a torture chamber. The images flashed in my mind forcing me to shiver. I didn't want to go inside, but I was never afraid of anything. Certainly, being a human wouldn't scare me away.

We began to make our way toward the house, trying to be quiet, but our steps were loud in the snow. Humans were always loud, no matter what. Elijah poised himself to be in the center of the group, so he could make us invisible. Gripping Alaric's hand, I tried ignoring the pounding of my heartbeat and the fear that seized me. What if Elijah was good at lying to demons and vampires? What if all of it was a setup?

As we entered the house, the scents of sage and lemon overwhelmed me.

"Stay close," Elijah whispered. "And don't make a sound."

I took a deep breath as we followed him down to a basement. The stairs creaked. Of course, they did. At the bottom of the stairs, we heard voices. It sounded like chanting in some foreign language. I didn't know what any of it meant. We stopped just outside a room that was filled with lit candles and a group of witches in black robes. Elijah turned to us with a finger across his lips and led the way down the hall. The room was familiar with the steel tables and empty buckets. The smell of blood was everywhere. Was it mine and Alaric's blood?

My feet planted to the ground, I didn't want to go back in that room.

"Why are we in here?" Alaric asked, clearly on edge.

Elijah twisted around with a stern look on his face. But why were we in the room? I didn't want to be here anymore than he did.

He opened a door that led to a secret stairwell. Alaric and I exchanged a look. Where was he taking us? He went first, then Lolly. Alaric and I followed. The concrete stairs narrowly wound their way into a cold and drafty room where Elijah made candles light up without a match. A part of me wanted to be a witch to be able to control things like that.

Once all the candles were lit, I scanned the room and saw that it was nothing but bookshelves full of books.

"Are these all their grimoires?" I whispered.

Elijah nodded. "The cures are here somewhere, too. We need to hurry."

"What spell are they chanting up there?" I asked.

"It's a locator spell or something."

I started looking for the cures, but Alaric crossed his arms and stared at Elijah. "You know exactly the spell they are chanting."

"What does it matter?"

His lack of honesty warned me, and I glared at Elijah. "What are you not telling us?"

"Jesus, you two are the most paranoid people I've ever met," Lolly said.

I moved closer to Elijah, pushing him against a shelf. "What spell is it?"

Elijah sighed. "They're channeling dark magic. They drink vampire blood and turn into vampires. That's why we need to hurry."

"What? What purpose?"

"They saved a lot of Alaric's blood. If one of them transitions to a vampire, they'll have his blood in their system. Then, they'll die in order to finish the ultimate spell."

"Aria is still alive, and they can't get to her."

"Don't underestimate the witches," Elijah said. "They can find her."

I swung my fist into his face. "Are you lying to us?" I yelled and immediately regretted it.

"Who's down there?" a voice asked.

Elijah made the candles blow out and we stood in the corner barely breathing. A large man with short blond hair walked down the stairs and lit the candles. Holding my breath, I gripped Alaric's hand, but as the man scanned the room, he saw nothing.

He scoffed. "Here for the cure, Elijah? You'll have to try a little harder than that."

We needed to torture the witches in order to gain the cure. I didn't think they would leave it anywhere unattended.

"You can't escape this. None of you can. And we know you killed Zeke. I guess you're okay knowing that he's dead, Elijah."

I stood without budging and held my breath. He had known Zeke was dead, but even when I admitted it to him, he didn't react much to the news. Did he not care about his brother?

Elijah snatched my hand, pushing me in front of him as if holding me hostage. "I know he died," he said, and the man stared at me. Elijah ratted us out, but when I glanced behind me, I couldn't see anyone. I guessed he just ratted me out. "She's the one who killed him."

I struggled against his grip, but he held me in place. I knew he couldn't be trusted. He had led us right back to the witches. It was all a trap.

"Yet, here you are helping her."

"Fat chance. I'm bringing her back for the sacrifice."

The man raised an eyebrow. "You know she's no good to us anymore, right?"

"She never transitioned all the way," Elijah said.

"Well then, let's bring her upstairs."

I heard Elijah's voice inside my head. *You have to kill him. Steal his dagger. It's inside his robe.*

I gave him a sideways glance and he nodded the tiniest bit.

My heart slammed into my chest and I took one breath before seizing the man's neck. He was huge, and my human self couldn't take him down, but as his back hit the wall, I punched him. Quickly lifting his robe, I found his dagger and snatched it. I didn't even see his fist coming toward my face. Pain shot through my head as I fell over. As a demon,

I was stronger than a witch or any man, but as a human, I felt vulnerable and feeble. I refused to lose the fight. Gripping the dagger in my hand, I swung it into whatever flesh I found first.

The man cried out, and Elijah pressed his hands to the man's head and his eyes rolled to the back of his head. The man collapsed to his knees and keeled over.

Breathing hard, I removed the dagger from the man's chest. "Where are the cures?" I threatened Elijah with the dagger.

"I just read his mind. They're upstairs in the séance room."

Alaric helped me to my feet. "Are you okay?"

I nodded, feeling awkward that a witch had just saved my life. I still didn't understand his motive, but I guessed we'd all find out soon enough. He didn't fight me or try to take the dagger away. I assumed he kept the others invisible and restrained them from helping me fight, probably so it wouldn't cause too much noise.

"Here's the bag," Elijah told Lolly, holding out a small satchel. "Fill it with all the grimoires."

"What are the rest of you going to do?"

"Looks like we're going to fight some witches for the cures."

CHAPTER THIRTY-NINE
ALARIC

Pride swelled in his chest as Alaric watched Harlow take down the witch. He had wanted to help, but Elijah had blocked them from interfering. He didn't know why he only had Harlow appear before the witch, but he was watching Elijah closer. Elijah led him and Harlow up the concrete stairs, and they paused right outside the séance room. They could've used some backup, but if the witches tried escaping, backup would kill them instantly. Alaric had to take some comfort in that. He'd hope Elijah hadn't just led them into another trap.

This will have to be fast, Alaric heard Elijah's voice in his head. *There are twelve witches in the circle. Harlow use the dagger. Alaric, the other witches have weapons on them. If you get to one fast enough, you can take it and use it. The Witches are strong and will not hesitate to use their magic. I will try to use as much magic as I can to hold them, but they are extremely strong now as they're bound.*

The thought of using a weapon was foreign to him. It had been so long since he had even thought about using one. He exchanged a determined look with Harlow and hoped like hell that it wasn't a setup. He would grab Harlow and get them out of there.

Elijah went in first and Alaric and Harlow followed. Alaric found the first witch and knocked him out. It seemed like Elijah stunned them all, but Alaric wasn't sure how long he could hold them. Alaric glanced back and saw blood trickling from his nose. They had to hurry.

Alaric seized a woman by the throat. She looked familiar, and he realized she was the witch who had helped Harlow the first time, Gemma. His vampire self wouldn't have hesitated for a second to kill, but guilt riddled his human self.

Grabbing her knife from her side, she cried out. "Please don't kill me! I was only following orders!"

One second, he faltered, and she murmured a spell that sent him flying across the room. He landed hard on his back. She tackled Elijah, breaking his hold on the other witches. Harlow was trying to fight off a man twice her size and she finally succeeded when she plunged the dagger right into his heart. Alaric removed any emotion and grabbed Gemma. He squeezed her neck until her face turned red. He didn't release her until her eyes began rolling in the back of her head. Her body crumpled to the floor and Alaric moved to the next witch.

Elijah, Harlow, and Alaric barely fought their way through seven of the witches. Two escaped and three joined in a circle.

Harlow rushed up to them, but an invisible force threw her against the wall. Anger filled inside Alaric, and he lunged for the witch, but they tossed him across the room. Elijah's hands lit in a blue flame and he surrounded the witches with it.

Within seconds, the witches collapsed in a heap of bodies. Alaric winced as he got to his feet and hurried over to Harlow. He lifted her unconscious body into his arms. The last time she'd been thrown against the wall, she was fine. They were humans now. Why were they still involved in the war? She had a point that they still belonged to the vampires and demons, but they couldn't keep fighting. Sure, revenge was a good motive, but was it worth risking their lives? They'd been given a second chance, and this was what they used it for?

"Harlow, wake up," he said.

"We need to get out of here. Ciara and Antony took the cures."

Fuck!

Alaric picked her up and carried her out of the psychotic witch's house behind Elijah, hoping she would wake soon.

CHAPTER FORTY
HARLOW

I was floating once again, yet my body throbbed and ached. The air was cold, but I was warm, and when I opened my eyes, I saw the most beautiful green.

"About time," Alaric said. "This really isn't the time for a nap."

I rolled my eyes. "I know. I was just resting my eyes."

"Can you walk."

"Yes." I could, but I didn't want to. Being in his arms made me feel safe. He eased me onto my feet and grabbed my hand. "What happened?"

"We killed most of the witches by some miracle. I think Elijah had a lot to do with it. Ciara and another witch escaped with the cures. Lolly was able to collect all of the grimoires."

"How are we going to find the cures? We need them for Grayson. I don't understand why they won't use one on Grayson."

"Who knows, but we need to get it out of their hands," Alaric said.

"Until one of them remembers the recipe for the cure and begins making them again."

"It's too complicated for memory," Elijah said.

We came up to a few shadows, and the closer we approached, I realized it was our group. My vision was terrible after the transition. Caleb, Mina, Danielle, and Sawyer held Ciara and Antony, but I wasn't sure how that was possible without them using powers. Estrella, and London stood idly by, waiting for them to attempt to make a move. Out of the corner of my eye, I saw more vampires and demons surrounding us. I hoped none of them were starving.

"We saw them running out," Caleb said. "This whole place is surrounded."

"Why aren't they using any powers?"

"I suspended their powers for a short time," Elijah said. "It won't last long."

"You won't win this war, Elijah," Ciara said. She wasn't afraid, and I knew she was just waiting until her powers returned. I had no idea that was a thing.

"Watch me." He glared at her and raised his hands. A blue light emitted from Ciara and drifted toward Elijah. Was he stealing her energy? Her life? Her powers?

"Stop!" Antony cried. "You don't want to do that."

Caleb released Ciara as she began floating toward Elijah. "What is going on?"

Antony struggled against Sawyer, but Sawyer had a good grip on him. "He's killing her."

"Where are the cures?" I demanded.

"You'll never find them. Why would you want to destroy them? You're a human. You have no say in this war any longer."

I marched up to him and slugged him in the face. "I may not be a demon anymore, but I sure as hell can still kill you." I seized his throat and squeezed.

"You've made your point, Harlow," Danielle said.

"No. He's going to suffer, just like he made us suffer. Where are the cures?"

"I will never tell you. Kill me all you want. At least I will have died for a great cause."

"Cause? You call genocide a great cause?"

"You're all monsters that deserve to die."

"And you're a part of the monsters who created us." I squeezed around his neck as hard as I could.

"Harlow, that's enough," Sawyer said.

But I ignored him. I heard a hard thud in the snow and felt hands on my arms.

"Harlow, let go," Alaric said. "Let Elijah finish the job."

"We can't kill him, Alaric," Danielle said. "We need him alive to show us where the cures are."

"I know exactly where the cure is," Elijah said. "But I need someone to carry the cure."

"What?" Danielle asked.

"I need someone now," he yelled.

"Fine, I'll do it," I said, whatever that meant.

Elijah stood next to me, taking my hand. "Let me handle this."

After a second, I finally released my grip on Antony. Elijah removed him from Sawyer's hands. "I'm so sorry it's come to this. But you should've known better than to trust me." He squeezed my hand, and suddenly I felt a power grow inside me. My ears rang as my blood pulsated. A strange burning sensation filled my insides and I cried out.

"Harlow, what is it?" Alaric asked. No one approached me or budged from their spots. Elijah mumbled words and refused to release my hand. I watched Antony's eyes roll to the back of his head and I couldn't stand up any longer.

My heart pounded as I fell to the ground. The cold snow felt great against my warm skin. I closed my eyes, wanting to sleep.

CHAPTER FORTY-ONE
ALARIC

Alaric couldn't move a single muscle until Harlow and Antony fell into the snow. It was as if something paralyzed him, and he knew exactly who did it.

"What the fuck was that?" Caleb asked.

Alaric rushed to Harlow's side. "I swear if you killed her, you will die."

"I didn't kill her," Elijah said, his body swaying. "She'll wake up in a few moments."

Danielle kneeled next to Antony, checking his pulse. "You just killed the one person who knows where the cures are."

"Are you okay?" Lolly asked Elijah.

"Fine. Just tired. I need rest." Elijah took a deep breath. "I need you all to listen closely. Antony was the cure."

"What?" Mina asked, folding her arms across her chest.

"The witches put the cure inside Antony. I couldn't very well keep him hostage and bring him to Grayson, so I transferred the cure into Harlow. Her blood contains the cure."

Alaric clenched his teeth and tackled Elijah. "What the fuck did you do?"

"Get off me and I'll explain."

He got to his feet and jerked Elijah to his, still gripping him by his collar. "You better explain fast or you're going to be someone's dinner."

"Harlow is strong enough to handle this. I transferred Antony's powers into her. Once we find Grayson, she will be able to convince him to drink her blood."

Alaric shook him. "You fucking asshole. She wasn't supposed to die."

"And she won't. You have to listen to me. When Grayson drains her of her blood, she will come back to life as I have sacrificed myself. You must have balance in the world for perfect harmony."

Lolly gasped. "What? Are you saying you're going to die when she wakes?"

"Once Grayson drinks her blood, yes."

Tears welled in her eyes. "No."

"This is the way it has to be, Lolly."

"What about the grimoires?" Sawyer asked. "Aren't you supposed to hide them and put a spell on the place? Won't that kinda be ruined once you die?"

"I'm the last of the coven. It's up to you all to hide them now."

"Don't you think you should've talked to us about all of this before you made the executive decision?" Alaric asked.

"I had to act fast. This was the only thing I could think of that would work."

"And you're sure Harlow will wake?"

"Yes."

"Why does she get to live and not you? Why do you have to be the one to sacrifice yourself?"

"Lolly, it'll be okay." He caressed her cheek.

Harlow moaned, and Alaric was at her side. She slowly opened her eyes and made a disgusted sound. "I'm so sick of passing out."

"But you get to see my face every time."

She rolled her eyes. "What the fuck happened?"

"I don't even know how to explain." He shook his head and told Harlow what they had all learned. He hated the scared look in her eyes, a look he'd never seen from her before.

"When's this sacrifice supposed to take place?" Harlow asked, her teeth chattering.

"Tomorrow night. Some of us need to rest before. Grayson's looking for the witches, so we're going to lead him to us," Elijah said.

Caleb crossed his arms. "And how do you suppose we do that?"

Elijah met Alaric's eyes. "You can lead him here."

"You're kidding, right? The second he sees me, I'm dead."

"If you go back and claim the witches kidnapped you and turned you into a human, you can build up the story that you want revenge."

Elijah had a point, and while he'd gotten his revenge already, he didn't want to leave Harlow again, not knowing if he'd ever see her again. He had already been separated from her once, and that had been enough. Alaric didn't know if he was strong enough to leave her again.

"There has to be another way."

"If any of us show our faces to Grayson, he will attack," Danielle said. "Seeing yours and realizing you're human will cause him to take a minute to listen. You won't be by yourself completely." She touched his arm, and Harlow glared at her. Alaric removed his arm from Danielle's touch.

"We will be here, waiting, but we can't send anyone else because Grayson and his hybrids will know it's a ploy," Elijah said.

"Why can't you go with him and protect him?" Harlow asked. "Use your invisibility like Zeke did with me."

"You and I are connected, Harlow. If something were to happen to me, it would happen to you."

"You never mentioned that." Alaric clenched his fists.

"Harlow can't die unless Grayson kills her. If she dies another way, then our plan of ending this war will cease and I won't resurrect."

"You aren't going to resurrect anyway." Lolly pouted.

Elijah took Lolly's hands in his. "I'm sorry for that."

Harlow shivered, and Alaric pulled her into an embrace, not ever wanting to let her go. They hadn't been together long, and it seemed like every time they tried being together, something was tearing them apart. He honestly didn't know if Grayson would believe him or spare his life, especially since he was a human, he could be compelled, or the hybrids could detect his lying.

Alaric didn't know what would come of them, but in that moment, he held Harlow as tight as he could, programming to memory her sweet jasmine scent. The way her body felt against his. The way she always held her ground. He even liked arguing with her and admired her strength. He would have nothing if she died. He would have no reason to live. He couldn't imagine his life without her.

CHAPTER FORTY-TWO
HARLOW

Returning to the witch's house, we immediately made a fire, and the four humans huddled next to it after Elijah prepared soup and bread for us. Hunger pangs were something to get used to again. The crackling and popping of the wood calmed me. I thought I had been saved from having to sacrifice myself, but I wasn't. And neither was Alaric. I hated knowing there was a chance I would never see him again. Would Grayson spare his life? Why would Grayson do that? Once Alaric led them back to the witch's house, why wouldn't he kill Alaric?

I gripped Alaric's hand, hating the heavy sickening feeling in my stomach. It made my stomach churn and I couldn't eat.

The witch's house reeked of blood, but the vampires and demons cleaned it up, as much as they could.

"Drink this." Elijah handed Alaric a glass of what looked like to be water.

"What's this?"

"It's water, but I've added an herb that helps prevent compulsion from vampires."

"Does it help against demons?"

"Not really, but this is the best thing. Drink this tonight and all day tomorrow."

"What about me?" I asked.

"You won't need it. I will be protecting you."

Lucky me. I couldn't believe we were putting all of our trust into this witch. He was the one to save us all. And for what? What exactly did he get out of it? "Why are you doing this?"

"If I don't, the hybrids will kill you."

"No, I mean, why are you doing all of this? Helping us take down Grayson, killing your own coven. You didn't even bat an eye when you found out I killed Zeke."

Elijah let out a breath. "My coven has tried to play god for too long. They created an entirely new species. Only because vampires bullied them. My hope is that if I help, the vampires will leave witches alone and all three can live in harmony. When I saw that vampires and demons were in cahoots together, I got the idea. Of course, I was sad about Zeke, but he took the domination a little too far. He wanted witches to be the rulers or whatever. But you all are the leaders. You can bring everything together and create order. The only thing I'm sad about is that I won't be around to see it, unless a witch calls upon me."

Lolly burst into tears. "This isn't fair."

"Nothing is fair."

Alaric stood and helped me to my feet. "Where can we sleep?"

"Past the séance room, you'll come to a grand staircase. Up the stairs is where you can stay."

He led me through the grandiose witch's house. It was quite ornate with large portraits on the walls. Despite it being a place where witches lived, it was rather warm. Warmer than what I remembered the Lair being like. Or maybe everything felt different to me now.

As we ascended the stairs, we chose a room at the end of the hall on the second story. We entered a room with a canopy bed, hardwood floors, and black furniture. All of it looked unused, even the bed looked unslept in.

"I wasn't expecting this," I said, easing down onto the bed.

"I'm not sure what I expected."

The bed sank as Alaric sat next to me, placing an arm around my waist. I rested my head on his shoulder. I didn't want it to be our last night together.

He lifted my chin, forcing me to look up at him. His green eyes gazed into mine, then his lips were on mine in an urgent, wanting manner. I slipped my hand beneath his shirt, feeling his soft skin, and I wanted him.

We didn't take our time removing our clothes, and within seconds, we were both under the covers staring at each other. Alaric kissed me again, and I felt his hard cock against my thigh. My body hummed and throbbed in places. He kissed his way down to my stomach and bent my knees. He licked my clit.

"I love the way you taste." Shoving his tongue inside my pussy, I moaned as heat enraptured me. Human or not, Alaric still knew how to please. He knew every little way to make me moan and thrust against his face. He kissed, licked, and nibbled my clit until I came.

Alaric sank his hard cock inside me as I wrapped my legs around him. His thrusts were slow and rhythmic, and I couldn't believe how good sex still felt. I didn't feel like ripping someone's head off. I didn't have to associate violence with sex. I focused on how good he felt inside me, hitting all the right places.

Gazing into my eyes, he held me close as he still pumped in and out of me. "I love you, Harlow. Always."

"I love you."

He kissed me hard. "Now, get on all fours."

I did, and he teased my nether region with his finger and slammed his cock inside my warmth. Again and again. He was rough, yet gentle. He slapped my ass and gripped my hips. I couldn't be quiet, and he felt so good.

He thrusted three, four times before he released his seed inside me.

Alaric and I relaxed in each other's arms, or as much as we could relax. We didn't say a word, because we knew no words could be spoken. Nothing would help ease the horror of tomorrow. Rest wouldn't come, even though we needed it, but I focused on his hand caressing my back. I had never imagined falling in love. Even before I became a demon, it never felt like it was something that would ever happen to me. I had always been too rigid, too selfish. But I had no choice as an orphaned girl, I had to do what was necessary to survive. Even when I became a demon. Love wasn't even a choice. Part of me wished I still didn't know what it was, because the pain was unbearable. How could I feel such sorrow over another person? Why did humans put so much stock into each other, knowing there was a possibility of losing them?

I knew why I did. Because being in love with Alaric trumped any grief I may experience. Even if it was just for a little while, at least I knew what love felt like, and it made all of the heartache, the fighting, everything worth it. He was the reason I kept going. And if we survived the war, he would still be that reason.

CHAPTER FORTY-THREE
ALARIC

As he held Harlow close against his chest, Alaric peered out the window at the sun. It barely crested above the horizon, and he knew the vampires and demons would be asleep for several more hours. He didn't sleep at all, and he knew he wouldn't. Not when he was hours from marching to his potential death.

He watched the sun rise, mesmerized by its beauty. The rich orange meshed with the purple of the sky creating a vibrant colored horizon. Dark clouds loomed like it knew what today would bring. He needed to sleep and get some rest, but what was the point? If Grayson decided to kill him, he had an entire army of hybrids ready to kill, and some measly human would take seconds. He could fight about two, maybe three, but there was no way he could take on the entire army. But he would try all he could, if it meant he'd see Harlow once more.

Alaric tried to sleep, but he woke up off and on. Harlow woke up, and whenever they were awake, they made love and held each other. The waiting was the hardest part.

Waiting to die. Waiting to go to war. The stagnant waiting. As the sun dipped below the horizon, the vampires and demons awakened.

Everyone had gathered in the main room of the witch's mansion. Harlow stayed close to Alaric as they waited for instructions. Alaric didn't exactly need instructions. He knew what he had to do. He wasn't nervous at all. He didn't know what he felt. Maybe that particular attribute of being a vampire had carried over to his human life. The ability to turn off emotions. He was good at it, even before becoming a vampire.

When Elijah finished reiterating what everyone needed to do, Alaric met his eyes. "You need to punch me. If I escaped the witches, I need to look like someone who got away."

Elijah nodded. "Very well." He swung his fist into Alaric's face. It jarred him for a second, but it was enough to draw blood.

Caleb ripped his shirt. "Just for good measure."

Alaric nodded, and looked around the room. He didn't do goodbyes, but he didn't miss the sad looks on Danielle and Lolly's faces. Sadly, he didn't care. He gave Harlow a quick kiss and bolted out the mansion into the freezing snowy night.

He had to fight through the cold, even though he wasn't entirely sure he knew exactly where Grayson's army was. Alaric trudged through no matter what. The snow was thick, reaching his knees. He wondered if it would ever stop snowing.

Light from the half moon cascaded over him and glittered along the snow. There was no way he could sneak up on the hybrid army, and he just hoped they wouldn't attack him immediately.

He traveled for what seemed like forever. His toes and fingers were frozen. His body shivered uncontrollably. Alaric didn't need to get frostbite. Being a vampire had had its advantages, especially when it was cold.

Slowing his pace, he saw in the distance a group walking toward him through the trees. His heart slammed into his chest. He knew he'd found Grayson.

As he moved closer, he hesitated. The army moved faster than he anticipated.

Grayson came to view and held up an arm. "Well, well, well. How ever did you manage to survive?"

"Barely."

Grayson squinted his eyes and tilted his head slightly. "It seems you are right."

Trajan moved to the front of the line. "You're a human?"

"You're smart."

"What happened to you?"

"Witches kidnapped me. Drained me of my blood and turned me into a human. I escaped, but I know where to find them if you want to kill them."

"You're willing to help us?" Grayson asked, cocking an eyebrow.

"I don't give a fuck who I help. Those fucking witches need to die. They've created a goddamn cure to vampirism and demonism."

Grayson held a cold look in his eyes. "Playing with fire, I see. And you're going to just lead us right to them?"

Alaric knew he was trying to compel him. "Yes. I will lead you right to them."

"Take us to these witches, then. I want this war to be over. But, a warning. If you're leading us into a trap, you'll be killed instantly."

"Not if the cold kills me first."

Grayson gave a quick chuckle.

"Why don't you become a vampire again?" Trajan asked.

"Hadn't really had the time to think about it, what with my blood being drained and all."

"The man just escaped," Grayson said. "There's no human blood for miles. Once we get to the witches, we'll save one for Alaric to turn again. We'll have him back into our army in no time. In the meantime, someone give him a coat or something. I can't have him die before we get there."

Alaric shivered as one of the hybrids obliged without argument. Fucking sire bond. Grayson must have been that insecure and lonely to create an entire army sired to him. They could never leave him or do anything against his word. How long had he expected that to last?

He didn't know how the rest of the plan was to unfold, since they could all hear heartbeats, but witches always covered themselves in some type of protection. He hoped they would protect him once they reached the hideout.

CHAPTER FORTY-FOUR
HARLOW

Minutes ticked by. And we waited. We waited so long I had imagined over a thousand ways Alaric died. But I had also imagined him returning and everyone lived happily ever after. If only. If I were a demon, I could reach out to Alaric's mind and talk to him there. I couldn't sit still. My stomach felt like something was crawling all over and nipping at my insides. Dmitry tried to comfort me, but I knew he was worried, too. We all were. About potentially dying or losing each other.

"I see them heading this way," Elijah called, and my heart tripped over itself.

"Is Alaric—"

"He's with them. The house is invisible to them."

"What? You have to make it appear," I screamed. "They'll kill him."

Elijah took my hand and mumbled something. Everything went dark, but I was still aware of what was going on. I could see, feel, but I had no control of my body or actions. It was as if I was possessed. Had Elijah gotten inside my head? We walked out of the hideout in the cold night. I knew, in a few hours, the sun would peak over the horizon.

I didn't like not being in control of myself. Elijah walked beside me, but he was invisible to Grayson and his army.

Alaric's eyes were trained on me as I approached Grayson.

In one second, I heard the footsteps in the snow, the quiet of the night, and in the next second, screams and bloodshed transpired. Hybrids knocked me down, but I was able to fight them off, as if I was still a demon. I didn't understand it, but maybe it was Elijah giving me power.

Scanning the area, I saw everyone clawing, punching, kicking, limbs being torn apart, tossing them into the air, but I couldn't find Alaric. I couldn't worry about him. I had a mission.

I saw Grayson tearing apart demons and vampires as if they were simply a feral cat. I needed to kill his hybrids before he would even glance in my direction. A hybrid lunged for me. I ducked and jammed my hand into the hybrid's chest, clutching his heart. I missed that feeling of complete control. Holding a man's beating heart and watching him squirm. Me, being the decider of his fate. As I held his slimy, bloody heart, I kicked him, and as he fell over, his heart pulled through his chest. I tossed the heart into the snow and continued killing the hybrids as they approached me.

Someone grabbed me from behind, tackling me to the ground. I turned over and his fangs protruded. His eyes turned black and then the familiar ruby red. I gasped. I never realized how scary the red eyes could be.

I struggled with him, trying to break free. He had more strength than I anticipated as he bared his fangs, conquering me. He snapped and nipped at my neck until his teeth grazed my throat. Blood tickled my neck as it trickled down. I would not die by a hybrid. I had to get to Grayson. Using more strength, I pushed him off me and got to my feet. Blood spurted from my neck as I became face to face with Grayson.

A sly smile stretched across his lips as his black eyes glared at me, then my bleeding neck. "You are one naïve demon. You think you can defeat me?"

The fuzzy darkness or whatever it was lifted from me, and his eyes widened.

His expression changed. "You're a human."

My heart pounded, and he could smell my blood. He stared at my neck like he was in a trance and couldn't be distracted.

He licked his lips and his fangs grew. Tilting his head back, he growled before sinking his teeth inside my vein. I winced from the puncture as fire spread all over me. It started out as an annoying ache, but the pain grew. Grayson drank and drank. Dizziness overwhelmed me, and I saw flashes of images. Images of me as a young girl. Of my family. Images of me becoming a demon. And then of Alaric.

Let go, Harlow. Live your life without any regrets and fulfill your wishes.

I knew it was Elijah's voice in my head, as death slowly enraptured me into its arms, cradling me into darkness.

CHAPTER FORTY-FIVE
ALARIC

One by one, the hybrids, demons, and vampires stopped fighting and watched as Grayson cried out next to Harlow's dead body. He writhed like some fucking crazed animal, spitting saliva from his mouth. Alaric knew exactly the pain Grayson experienced. He was transitioning into a human, and it also meant he was the cure.

"What the fuck is going on?" Trajan asked as he stared, wide-eyed at Grayson. He was panting, like the rest of them. "Something…something's different."

Danielle hesitated toward Trajan. "Do you feel different? Feeling less likely to want to kill me for harming Grayson?"

Trajan looked up, meeting her eyes. "Fuck, Dani. I'm so sorry." They embraced and kissed like they'd been apart for centuries.

Alaric rolled his eyes. Well at least someone got a happy ending.

"You are no longer sired to Grayson," Caleb announced to the hybrids. Alaric was impressed with the way he held himself, the true king of the vampires. "Things are going to change around here." Mina took his hand in hers and they exchanged a simple smile.

Aria, shaken and bleeding across her face, weakly made her way into Dmitry's strong arms.

Harlow still didn't move, and once Caleb picked up Grayson by the neck, Alaric rushed to Harlow's side. What was it about the two of them constantly passing out? Except she wasn't unconscious. She was dead. But she would wake. He had to keep reminding himself.

Elijah's body had appeared as soon as Harlow lost consciousness. The house became visible and Lolly ran outside kneeling beside Elijah.

As Alaric held Harlow's body, staring at her beautiful skin, aching for her eyes to open, he did everything he could to not let his emotions show. There hadn't been a guarantee she would return. Why had she agreed so willingly to carry the cure?

He looked up and when he saw Sawyer holding Caroline, his heart ached. Caroline didn't survive. And neither did several other hybrids, vampires, and demons. It had been a hard-fought war. The snow was covered in blood and body parts and dead bodies.

The sky began to lighten, and everyone began to retreat inside the witch's hideout. Alaric lifted Harlow, wishing she would wake up. He didn't know how long it would take, but he wasn't sure how he could wait any longer.

Taking her to the room they shared the night before, he lay her on the bed and stroked her soft blonde hair and waited. He tended to her wounds, closing up the nasty cut on her neck and the puncture wounds from Grayson. Her skin appeared gray and dead-like. Alaric took deep breaths and held back his emotions but seeing her in that state was killing him. He felt sick.

"She will wake up, you know." He heard Danielle from the doorway.

"I know. You and Trajan make up?"

"We did. Thanks. You're an amazing man, Alaric. Don't ever forget that."

"Is this a goodbye?"

"Trying to. It isn't easy."

"You think Harlow and I will leave or something?"

She furrowed her eyebrows. "You're human, now. You and Harlow can't be among us any longer."

"Wasn't that what the whole war was about? Coming together? We proved ourselves."

"I know. I just meant wouldn't it be awkward?"

"Harlow and I can manage just fine."

Danielle nodded. "I'll leave you two alone." She closed the door, and Alaric slipped onto the bed next to Harlow, watching the sun rise. It wasn't the same though, since Harlow wasn't awake to see it. He wanted her to wake so that they would have a lifetime of sunrises to watch together. A lifetime of love. Time had slowed down since they'd become human, and he wanted to enjoy every moment he could, because it wouldn't last forever.

She stirred, and Alaric released a breath. Her skin tone was no longer gray, it was the beautiful pale color he loved. She was beautiful, and his heart stilled at the sight.

"Fuck you scared me." He gazed into her brown eyes, but something was off. "Harlow?"

"Who-Who are you?"

"What?" That fucking witch never mentioned amnesia. How could she not remember him? Granted, she had died and was reborn.

A cunning smile stretched her lips. "You're so gullible."

Shaking his head, he leaned down and pressed his lips to hers, knowing that she would forever be a demon.

EPILOGUE
HARLOW

Coffee had become such a staple in my life, as ridiculous as that sounded. I poured two cups, one for me, and one for Alaric. We lived in a loft in the city with large gaping windows, like Alaric's apartment he had as a vampire, or the one he described to me. We were on the fifteenth floor, and as I looked out the window at the beautiful sunrise, I was reminded of all the times he fucked me in front of the window.

I sipped my coffee and heard him padding down the hall.

"Good morning Mrs. Kingston." He wrapped his arms around me and I inhaled his fresh shower scent.

"Good morning. I made coffee."

"Mmm, I think I want breakfast first." He nuzzled my neck and kissed me right behind the ear, sending warm chills across my skin, immediately turning me on.

"We can't be late." I placed my coffee onto the end table next to us, and reached behind me, rubbing his erection. "We have a meeting—"

"My cock has a meeting with your pussy." He slipped his hand inside my panties through the slick folds of my pussy. He growled and removed my panties. Lifting my leg slightly, he slid his hard length inside me.

Moaning, I balanced myself against the windows, leaving handprints that we'd clean later.

"Goddamn Harlow, you feel fucking amazing." He slapped my clit as he pumped inside me in a fast rhythm. Heat poured over me as he vigorously rubbed my clit. Knowing people could possibly see us turned me on as well.

"Don't stop," I begged, and he sped up his movements.

The orgasm released, and my body almost fell limp as he slammed his hard cock inside me. Seconds later, his orgasm followed.

"Who needs coffee when you have an amazing breakfast?" he asked, breathless. He kissed me and slapped my ass as he pulled out of me. "I love you."

"I love you."

We dressed and headed to work. Pulling into the parking deck of one of the finance buildings downtown, we parked and took the elevator to the twenty second floor. Alaric kissed me, and we entered Noble Financial. He had taken on the role of vice president of marketing, while I worked as a vice president of something. Vampires and Demons had joined together and created a consultant company that had quickly taken off as an up and coming company. People flocked to use our services.

Life was different, but it seemed to have more meaning, and Alaric and I appreciated it more. Work was actually fun, something I was good at. I didn't miss killing or having to kill in order to survive. I ate food to survive.

On Fridays, we went out with our friends and family to the new Underground. We were untouchable to the vampires, and everyone knew not to touch us. We'd gone out after work, and as usual it was nice to see Mina and Caleb together and Trajan and Dani. Of course, there would always be certain things I would miss about being a demon.

But as time went by, it felt like a past life, and slowly I didn't miss it.

I held Alaric's hand as the waiter came by to take our drinks.

"Vodka tonic," Alaric said.

"I'll have cosmo—"

"She'll have a water," Danielle said.

I looked at her, confused. "What?"

"You don't need to be drinking alcohol."

"Why? What's wrong?" I asked.

Danielle lowered her eyes to my stomach. "I can hear another heartbeat."

Alaric and I exchanged a look and his warm smile reached his beautiful green eyes. We could now carry on our family legacy. I never thought it was possible, but I had a family again, and vampires and demons would live on forever in harmony.

THE END

ABOUT THE AUTHOR

C.J. Hartnett spends her days writing dark stories with a bit of naughtiness. She is a horror enthusiast, loves to cook for her family, and thoroughly enjoys gardening.